When a sailboat carrying four bodies washes up on the Leeward Coast of O'ahu, openly gay Honolulu homicide detective Kimo Kanapa'aka, on loan to the FBI, must discover what sent this young family and their deadly cargo on a dangerous trans-Pacific voyage. Leaving behind his partner and their infant twins, Kimo must work with his police cohort Ray Donne to unravel the forces that led this family to their deaths. From Hawaii's sunny beaches to a chillly island in Japan to the Pacific Northwest, Kimo and Ray step far out of their comfort zones to confront an evil much greater than any they've investigated before.

Ghost Ship
A Mahu Investigation

Neil S. Plakcy

Published by
MLR Press, LLC
3052 Gaines Waterport Rd.
Albion, NY 14411

Visit ManLoveRomance Press, LLC on the Internet:
www.mlrpress.com

Editing by Kris Jacen

Print format: ISBN# 978-1-944770-34-1
ebook format also available

Issued 2016

Trademarks Acknowledgment

The author acknowledges the trademark status and trademark owners of the following wordmarks mentioned in this work of fiction:

Alcoholics Anonymous: Alcoholics Anonymous World Services, Inc.

Bluetooth: Bluetooth Sig, Inc.

BMW: BMW of North America, Inc.

Cornell: Cornell University

Corvette: General Motors

Doogie Howser: 20th Century Fox Television and Steven Bochco Productions

FedEx: FedEx

Glock: Glock, Inc.

Google: Google, Inc.

Greenpeace: Greenpeace USA

Groundhog Day: Columbia Pictures

Harvard: President and Fellows of Harvard College

Hawaiian Air: Hawaiian Airlines

Hello Kitty: Sanrio Co., LTD

Honolulu Community College: University of Hawaii

IBM: International Business Machines Corporation

Jeep: Chrysler Group LLC

Lawrence Livermore Labs:

MIT: Massachusetts Institute of Technology

PETA: People for the Ethical Treatment of Animals

Pokémon: Pokémon/Nintendo

Punahou: Punahou School

Rolodex: Berol Corporation

Skirokiya: Shirokiya International

Skype: Skype Limited Corporation

Speedos: Speedo Holdings B.V.

University of Hawai'i: University of Hawaii

University of Washington: University of Washington

Zippy's: Zippy's, Inc.

Dedication

To the members of my awesome critique group: Chris Jackson, Kris Montee and Sharon Potts. The book wouldn't be as good without your help.

1 – Barking Sands

A blue and white sailboat with three sails rested on its side against a rocky shoreline, a gaping hole in the port bow. The sparse grass along the shore had been blocked off by yards of yellow hazard tape, and a rough surf smashed against the hull. In the distance I could see a surfer cresting the top of an early morning wave.

"Turn up the TV volume," I said to my partner, Mike. We were watching *Wake Up, Honolulu!*, the morning news program on KVOL, the scrappy independent TV station in Honolulu where my brother Lui worked. It had become our habit now that we were empty-nesters, with our foster son Dakota a sophomore at the University of Hawai'i and living on campus. The twins we had fathered four years before lived with their moms, a lesbian couple who were our close friends, and came to visit us on alternate weekends, or whenever their moms needed a break.

Mike raised the volume in time for us to hear the perky female anchor say, "A jogger on the Leeward Coast made a gruesome discovery just after dawn this morning. Police are already on the scene but have declined comment."

She turned to face the camera. "And now, let's take a look at the newest baby otter at the Honolulu Zoo!"

"You can lower the volume now," I said.

"I'm at your service, master," Mike said with a grin. Mike was half-Italian and half Korean, while my parents had passed down Caucasian, Japanese and Hawaiian strains. We both had skin that tanned easily, dark hair and facial features that identified us as mixed race, though he was a few inches taller than I was.

Cathy and Sandra, the mothers of our twins, had worked out a scheme which we went along with. Mike's and my sperm were mixed with Cathy's eggs, and the resulting embryos had been implanted into Sandra's womb. That way all four of us were participants in their birth. The twins looked like a mix of all of us—just as we'd hoped.

While Mike finished getting dressed I made sure that our golden retriever, Roby, had water and toys to play with while we were at work. Before we walked out, we stopped at the front door for a goodbye kiss—another of our newer rituals.

Mike was a fire investigator with the Honolulu Fire Department, evaluating any suspicious blazes and teaching his colleagues about new techniques in arson evaluation. My job was no less dangerous than his—after years as a street patrolman and then homicide detective with the Honolulu Police Department, I'd gone on assignment to the FBI's Joint Terrorism Task Force.

We'd both made a pact years before never to leave each other angry, not knowing what the day could bring. And with Dakota out of the house, we'd indulged in the kind of hot, deep kisses that sealed our desire for each other. Mike grabbed my ass and leaned down, pressing his lips against mine in a clash that grew hotter as we pressed together.

My dick popped up and strained against my pants, and I panted with desire. "I don't have to be at work on time this morning," I said, arching my head back so Mike could nip at my neck. "How about you?"

He unbuttoned the white dress shirt I had begun to wear when I joined the FBI. Mike was wearing a polo shirt with the HFD logo on the breast, so it was easy to pull the tails out of his slacks and stick my hands underneath, sliding through his silky chest hairs.

He unbuckled my belt and unhooked my pants, and they fell to the floor. My dick popped out of the slit in my tropical-print boxers and he wrapped his hand around it as we exchanged hot, sinful kisses.

My cell phone rang as I undid his pants and shoved them to the tile floor. "Let it go," Mike growled into my neck, and I ignored the call—and also released his dick from his briefs.

We kept kissing as we jerked each other in hard, fast strokes. My heart raced and my orgasm rose, suffusing my body with an energy so strong I thought I must be glowing. Then I came, spurting into his hand, and he followed a moment later.

Our bodies sagged together, and I reached out for the front door to steady myself. "Still got it, babe," Mike said.

My phone beeped to announce a new voice mail, but I ignored it. Mike and I were a tangle of pants around our ankles and sticky come on our hands, and it took a few minutes to extricate ourselves and clean up. Then we kissed goodbye again—this time just a quick peck on the cheek—and I walked out to my Jeep.

It was a gorgeous day in the islands, just a few clouds striating the blue sky, a light breeze dancing in the palm fronds. As I got onto the highway, a broad-winged bird soared high above the highway, and I wished I could be that free—if I didn't have to go to work, I'd have been out on the surf beyond that wrecked sailboat.

Then I remembered that missed call and voice mail. I turned the Bluetooth on and heard the voice of my detective partner, Ray Donne. "Need you here ASAP," he said. "We've got a meeting in the small conference room as soon as you get in."

I hit the gas and zoomed around a convertible full of tourists taking pictures of the scenery with their cell phones. When I got to the office, Ray was waiting for me.

He and I were like brothers from another mother. We'd worked together for nearly nine years by then, at HPD and the FBI. He was a couple of inches shorter than my six-one, his hair was wavy brown and mine straight black, and he was stockier than I was. But over time we'd developed the ability to read each other's thoughts and finish each other's sentences.

We hurried down the hall together. The conference room was set up with a dozen chairs auditorium style, all except two in the front occupied. Francisco Salinas, a tall, tanned Cuban-American guy with wavy dark hair and perennially pressed white shirts, stood by the podium, talking to a pair of agents I didn't know.

Ray and I had worked with Salinas on a couple of cases back when we were homicide detectives, and he'd requested our assignment to the JTTF, comprised of members of various law enforcement agencies who worked on Federal cases, with all the rights and privileges of special agents. At first, I'd been resistant, but over time I'd come to enjoy the diversity of cases Ray and I were able to work on, as well as the sense that occasionally what we did helped protect our country.

"The SAC is in DC," Salinas began, letting us know that the Special Agent in Charge had gone to our nation's capital. One of the things I hated about working with the Feds was the endless alphabet soup—the POTUS and FLOTUS (president and first lady) and so on. I often wondered if there was some Acronym Nomenclature of the United States, or ANUS, that we'd have to stick our noses into.

"I'm in charge until he returns," Salinas continued. "We've got a hot case that's unfolding right now, and I'm going to need all of you on it right away."

Besides Ray and me, the team Salinas had assembled included agents from Evidence Recovery, Field Intelligence, High Tech Crimes, and the High Intensity Drug Trafficking Task Force. There was also a language specialist and an analyst liaison to the Japanese embassy.

The last two intrigued me. In the four years Ray and I had spent at the Bureau we rarely interfaced with foreign language specialists. What kind of case was this?

The team also included a woman from Immigrations and Customs Enforcement and a guy from the Coast Guard. Salinas motioned toward the guy in the white uniform shirt. "Zach, since your agency were the first responders, you want to kick things off?"

Zach Hessler was a tall, slim haole—or white guy, with the sides of his head shaved, leaving just a bristle at the top. In his early forties, the epaulets on his shoulders identified his rank as a Lieutenant JG. He had a military bearing and I almost expected him to salute Salinas as he stepped over to a laptop on a podium.

He brought up an aerial photo of a beach on the big screen

behind him and I recognized the boat crash I had seen on TV that morning. The time stamp on the photo of the boat and surrounding area read 7:14 AM.

"This is an area just south of Ohikilolo Beach Park on the Leeward coast," he said. "Sometimes called Barking Sands— not to be confused with the missile base on Kauai." He used a laser pointer to indicate the boat. "At approximately 0500 hours this morning, the Coast Guard received a report of a sailboat that had crashed into the shore."

He clicked and the screen shifted to a closer view of the boat. I knew a bit about sailboats, from a life spent around the water, and I followed as he indicated the sails. "This sail here is on the main mast," he said, pointing. "This one here is attached to the forward stay— for those of you without a nautical background that means a wire fastened to the hull which supports the mast and controls how much it bends."

Then he pointed to the third sail. "This boat is what we call cutter-rigged that means it has an additional forward stay with this triangular jib attached to it."

He smiled. "Sorry for all the lingo, but it's important to recognize because all this equipment means the boat was prepared for long-distance sailing. With this combination of sails, an experienced captain can keep going in light or strong winds, which makes it possible it traveled all the way across the Pacific to reach us."

Another screen, this one a photo of a metal box with a nuclear hazard warning as well as extensive writing in Japanese. "Our first responders boarded the vessel and found this box on board, which further supports the hypothesis that the port of origin was somewhere in Japan."

I had learned a bit of spoken Japanese to communicate with Ojisan, as I called my Japanese-born grandfather, and I had taken four years of Japanese in high school. But whatever knowledge I had of *kanji*, the written language, had faded. I could recognize restaurant items and some street signs, but that was about it. The nuclear hazard symbol on the box, the yellow circle containing the three black triangles, was the same in any language.

Hessler pointed at a series of characters. "These ideograms mean Fukushima Dai-Ichi. The nuclear power plant on the Japanese island of Honshu, which was severely damaged during the earthquake and tsunami back in 2011. First responders called in our Hazmat team, which removed the box." He paused. "The responders also found four deceased individuals on board. Because of the possibility of nuclear contamination, the bodies are still in place."

He stepped down, and Salinas took his place. "The box was transported to our Hazmat facility, where the contents are under investigation right now. Unfortunately, because we have a couple of agents in training and we're involved with a hazardous waste site on the North Shore, our Hazmat teams are short-staffed. I've had to call in a favor from the Honolulu Fire Department and ask them to take over management of the site. Fortunately they have a Hazmat specialist they can spare."

I immediately thought of Mike, who was one of several with Hazmat experience in his department. Would he be there? I hoped not, because I didn't like the idea of him anywhere near nuclear contamination, even though I knew he was trained to deal with it.

Salinas put the pointer down. "We need to begin an immediate investigation into the individuals on board, the source of the nuclear material, and the intentions of those involved."

He ran through our assignments. An agent from Forensics would manage the Evidence Recovery Team, and another from the Cyber Task Force would get hold of the boat's navigational computer and figure out where it had come from and where it had been headed. An agent from High-Tech Intelligence would investigate suspected terrorists on the island who might have an interest in nuclear materials.

Then Salinas turned to Ray and me. "Since you gentleman have such extensive experience with dead bodies, you'll be going out to the site to liaise with the Medical Examiner and our brethren in the Coast Guard and the HFD."

We dispersed and Ray and I walked back to our office. "You

know where this place is?" he asked.

"General idea. We head up Farrington Highway and stop when we see the flashing lights and yellow tape."

Ray drove and I navigated, past the housing for Barber's Point Naval Air Station, flat land with mountains looming in the background, the suburban sprawl scattered with swaying palms and wind-twisted kiawe trees. The blue skies of earlier that morning were gone, and dark-bellied cumulous clouds loomed ahead of us.

That's not unusual—because of our mountainous geography, O'ahu is an island of micro-climates, and you could go from sun to showers to a full-on tropical downpour in a matter of minutes.

We got onto Farrington Highway, which quickly shifted from an interstate (yes, the Feds require us to call our highways interstates in order to get funding) to a divided four-lane with traffic lights and business driveways. Squat cabbage palms and spikes of pink ginger lined the road. We followed a pickup with a bumper sticker that read, "Sleep well, America, my Marine has your back."

It began to drizzle as we passed the broad white sands of Makaiwa Beach Park. Through the rain, we saw glimpses of the Pacific to our left, beyond the old sugar cane railroad. On Sundays, a diesel locomotive pulled tourists there in open cars for about six miles along the shoreline.

The tracks beside us ran out, and we passed through lots of open area—flat scrub to our right, rocky shore to our left. But soon enough outcroppings of development popped up—fast food, auto tint shops, a Head Start program and a Samoan Methodist Church. The rain intensified as we entered Ma'ili, a smaller outpost with a beachfront park and the Holy Hill of Zion Full Gospel church. It was a side of the island tourists rarely saw, without the glittering hotels of Waikiki or the towering surf of the North Shore. It was just a place where people lived.

After Ma'ili, we were back on a wild stretch of highway. By then the downpour had turned into a sheeting rain, and we were almost on top of the emergency vehicles before we saw their flashing lights. Ray pulled to a stop along the verge behind the ME's van.

We sat in the car waiting for the monsoon to pass. A pickup towing a sailboat crept past us, wipers flapping, and then suddenly the rain slowed to a drizzle and a rainbow appeared ahead of us. They're such a common phenomenon in the islands that the University of Hawai'i named their sports teams the Rainbows. Once the rainbow became a gay symbol, the administration tacked "Warriors" on to the end of the male teams. Then they figured out that made them sound like a bunch of radical gay activists, and they allowed each team to choose its own nickname. The result was a mishmash of Rainbows, Warriors, and Rainbow Warriors.

As Ray and I approached the yellow hazard tape around the sailboat in the light rain, someone in a bulky Hazmat suit climbed awkwardly off the bow, looking like a giant lime-green marshmallow man with a gas mask and bright yellow shoes. Even in that getup, I recognized the man I'd been sharing my life with for almost ten years.

Mike stepped onto a polyethylene walkway, stretched out his arms, and let the rain wash over him. The shower dissipated and the sun peeked out from behind the clouds. A guy in a firefighter's uniform stepped up to him, staying outside the yellow tape, and ran a long-handled scanner up and down the hazmat suit.

Mike was stepping out of the suit when I reached him. We tried to stay professional when we were working—no sweetheart, or honey, and that was difficult because I was worried about what he might have been exposed to on that boat.

I struggled to stay cool. "Hey. You find anything interesting in there?" I asked.

"Four dead bodies." Mike looked grim. "Two of them little babies. They look like Addie and Owen did at that age."

I could see why he looked shaken. The birth of our twins had rocked our worlds, bringing home the joy and the terror of parenting, and everything that happened to kids reminded us of how fragile those two little lives were.

2 – Little Angels

After chasing homicide cases for so long, I knew there were dozens of motives for killing an adult—but who could have taken the lives of those two infants on the sailboat in front of us? Had someone gotten on board, killed them all, then set it adrift?

In the now-brilliant sunshine, I stood beside the yellow hazard tape and looked at Mike, hoping he had some answers. "Is there a lot of blood?" I asked.

He shook his head. "It's almost creepy, how they're all dead but there's no sign of violence. I keep seeing those two little babies, looking so peaceful. Just like Addie and Owen."

I didn't know what to say. Mike rarely saw dead bodies in the course of his investigations. Either they'd been burned beyond recognition, or they'd been removed before he began his analysis of the way the fire had begun and spread. Over the years, I'd seen way too many bodies in all conditions, from so recently dead that blood was still flowing, to corpses in advanced states of decay. The sense of a life snuffed out still bothered me, but I had managed to compartmentalize those feelings and focus on bringing justice to the dead.

I took a breath. "When can we get on board to look around?" I asked.

"You can go on now, but you're going to have to suit up," Mike said. "I'm no ME, but it looks to me like they were all killed by exposure to whatever was in that container the Coasties took away." He shook his head. "K-Man, you can wear this one. There's another by the truck for Radon."

"I love the way he has pet names for everybody," Ray grumbled. "You're a superhero, and I'm a toxic gas."

"If the shoe fits," I said, and Ray poked me in the side.

By then, Mike had stepped over the yellow tape and stripped down to a one-piece zip-up jumpsuit, which he'd unzipped halfway down his hairy chest. I was glad we'd cleaned up well earlier, so no tell-tale traces of semen remained caught in his fur.

The firefighter with the scanner handed Mike a plastic bag with his clothes. He led me to a sheltered area around a rocky outcropping and began to step out of the jumpsuit. Ray went off with the scanner guy to get the other suit.

"You didn't disturb anything, did you?" I asked Mike as I watched him. It was strange that I'd seen his body less than an hour before, under such different circumstances.

"Coasties already removed the box with the nuclear symbol," Mike said. "And they took down the sails. All I did was trudge through the narrow space in this monster suit."

"It's tight in there?"

"It's a sailboat, K. Of course it's tight. The box containing the nuclear material was under the V-berths, so the radiation levels are highest back there. The whole boat is bad, but that's the worst." He handed the jumpsuit to me. "Strip down, sailor."

I followed his directions and began climbing into the suit he had so recently vacated. The suit was uncomfortably warm but I wasn't going to be a wuss and complain. After all, we'd just shared bodily fluids, so what was a little hot air between lovers?

"Will I be able to remove evidence from the boat? Or is it all going to be radioactive?"

"I wouldn't take anything from the V-berths. But as long as you don't touch anything to your skin, you should be able to handle the evidence and bring it ashore, though it should always be handled with gloves."

It took a half hour to get into the suits, and by then the sun was glinting off the waves and the air was super-heating. I was drenched in sweat before I even put the gas mask on over my head.

It was hard to move around in the bulky suit, and I felt like one of those astronauts on the moon, only without the benefit of zero gravity. As I approached the sailboat, I saw a cartoon drawing of a rabbit painted on the transom, above the name *Usagi Maru* in Roman script. I assumed that the kanji characters below the name meant the same thing.

I grabbed hold of the boat so I could step on board, and it shifted on the rocks. Great. All I needed was for it to take off while I was on board. I was an excellent swimmer but doubted I could do very well encased in protective layers.

Ray followed me on board. I went below first to begin combing the boat for clues while he looked around up on deck.

I began with the same basic questions I had in a homicide investigation, with a couple of twists. Who were these people, what were they doing with radioactive material, and how had they ended up on the rocks?

If the two adults were dead, who had steered the boat to shore? An autopilot? But when I squeezed into the cockpit, I discovered that all the electrical systems had been shut down. I poked around until I found the wind vane, which had been set with the coordinates of Pearl Harbor. The wind vane would have used the boat's main rudder, and the power derived from the motion of the boat through the water, to hold a constant angle to the wind. It was a kind of dead man's switch, something a sailor could use when he wasn't able to handle the boat himself.

My digital camera was awkward to use through the gloves, but manageable. I took pictures from every angle, though I wasn't sure what good it would do. There was no evidence that another party had come on board, and it was going to be nearly impossible to get a crime scene team in there because of the hazards from the radiation. I just knew that I didn't want to ever get back on that boat, so I had to collect anything I could.

In the cockpit, I found a captain's log which showed the boat had left Hakodate in northern Japan on a course through the north

Pacific with an eventual destination of the Elliott Bay Marina in Seattle. How had they ended up on the western shore of O'ahu instead? I didn't want to waste time on board reading the log so I stuffed it in one of the big pockets of the hazmat suit.

The situation reminded me of one of those locked-room mysteries I read when I was a teenager. No evidence of an intruder— so how had these four people died? Our initial read was radiation exposure, but how and why were still to be resolved. And especially, why hadn't that box been properly secured?

I found a photo album and some official papers in Japanese that I assumed were the boat's registration. It all went into zippered pockets. Then I squeezed through the narrow corridor and joined Ray in the main salon. It was about ten feet long, with a dark blue slip-covered settee along two sides under a lacquered wood table. Two baby seats sat at opposite ends, strapped to the settee.

The galley was along the far side, with pots and pans hanging from hooks on the wall. Clean dishes were in the drying rack, a book of charts propped up on a stand with the page opened to the waters around O'ahu. It looked eerie, like the houses in Pompeii after they were excavated from beneath the ash.

It was awkward being inside that suit, because three of the senses I used while investigating crime scenes were useless. I couldn't smell anything, hear anything or feel anything beneath my feet or my fingertips. At least I didn't usually use the sense of taste around dead bodies.

Ray opened a cabinet and pulled out two Juki Net cards, the ones Japanese nationals and foreign residents use for ID. Though most of the information was in kanji, the name Dale Griffin was in Roman script beside a photo of a Caucasian male with thinning blond hair. The other card was for a female, Chikako Griffin, a Japanese woman with long black hair and expressive dark eyes.

I left Ray snooping in the salon and turned sideways to step around the corner and into the cabin, where the two adult bodies rested in the queen-sized bed. Their skin was extremely pale, and they looked drawn and overly thin.

Dale appeared to be in his early thirties. He rested face up on top of the covers, his head turned toward Chikako beside him. He wore a grubby T-shirt with the logo of a Japanese beer company, plaid board shorts and scuffed deck shoes.

Chikako was a few years younger than Dale, maybe in her mid to late twenties, and she'd been tucked lovingly beneath the covers, with her long black hair splayed against the white pillowcase. She had an oval face that was pretty even in repose, and seemed smaller than she was by contrast to her big husband.

The cabin was sparsely decorated with tourist posters of Mount Fuji and a Buddhist temple. The door to the closet was open, and inside it I could see men's and women's clothes hanging neatly.

I took pictures of everything I could without disturbing the scene or the position of the bodies. It was awkward to lean in to get close-ups of the two adults, and despite all my experience around the dead I felt worse than usual, as if the bulky suit between me and the Griffins added an extra layer of distance that was disrespectful.

I sidled back through the salon to the narrow V-berth at the hull. A crib had been fixed to each side of the wall. And in each lay a baby, eyes shut and a blanket tucked beneath each chin. The boy's blanket was a pale blue with an ivory satin border; the girl's was pink with the same trim.

Seeing those babies tore at my heart, and I had to close my eyes for a moment to regain my composure. There was no blood anywhere, no sense that these tiny lives had suffered violent ends. I took a couple of deep breaths and then let the camera see what I couldn't bear to look at. By the time I was done my eyes were tearing behind the mask, and I didn't know which upset me more— that I couldn't wipe them, or the way those little angels resembled my own kids.

3 – Sunset Cruise

I stumbled back to the salon and up the short flight of steps to the deck. Ray was already on shore, where Mike was scanning him for radiation levels. Once Mike gave him the thumbs up, I stepped off the boat, eager to get the crime scene behind me. It was early afternoon by then, and I was hot, sweaty and sick to my stomach.

Ray and I both emptied our pockets, and everything we had pulled off the boat was scanned to make sure it wasn't toxic. Then we put each item into an evidence bag. By then, Doc Takayama, the Medical Examiner, was there with his techs. Doc graduated from medical school in his early twenties and went into pathology to avoid Doogie Howser comments from patients. Now that he was in his thirties he wasn't quite so baby-faced anymore.

Ray and I stood on the shore with him, watching the bodies being carried off the boat. His staff's procedures were slow and painstaking, as they were much closer to the bodies. "Will you have to do the autopsy inside one of those suits?" I asked him.

"There's a Hazmat-equipped suite at Tripler," he said. That was the Army hospital where Mike's parents had both worked, his father as a doctor and his mother as a nurse, until their retirement a year before. "I should be able to test for whatever trace elements are still in the bodies, and then calculate backwards to give you a rough time of death. I can tell you right off that the babies would have died first, because they have the smallest body mass. Then a couple of days later, the woman, and finally the man a few days after that."

"And all of it happened while they were at sea?" I asked. "I mean, the man was dead before the boat crashed into the shore, right?"

"From the position of his body I'd say that's correct."

There was nothing more for us to do there, so Ray and I walked down to the road, where Mike leaned against his truck conferring with a pair of EMTs. All the official vehicles were gone except for a single HFD emergency vehicle.

As we walked up, he shook hands with the two guys. "Give us a minute," he said to them.

They walked back toward their vehicle, and I said, "I hate the idea of going back to work like this. I feel like crap."

"Well, you won't have to go back so soon," Mike said. "I want to make sure we're all good and decontaminated. I had the local chief call in a favor, and those guys are going to take us down to a motel in Nanakuli where you, Ray and I can all shower and change into some scrubs graciously provided by the EMTs."

"Is it really necessary?" I asked. "You scanned us, didn't you?"

"I did. But I think it's worth going the extra mile when it's your health and mine at risk."

"Don't forget about me," Ray grumbled.

"Hey, buddy, my partner is your partner," he said. "Share and share alike."

Ray snorted. "Tell that to my wife."

We climbed into the back of the EMT bus and sat on the benches on the sides, holding on as it turned. When it stopped and we heard the engine shut off, Mike popped open the back door.

We stepped into the parking lot of a one-story motel a block from the ocean. A portly Hawaiian woman with a flowered muumuu and a collection of plastic leis around her neck came out of the office and handed us a card key for one of the rooms.

"Thank you ma'am," Mike said. "We appreciate it."

"Anything for my boys in blue," she said, reaching up to squeeze his cheek. Ray and I turned away to snicker.

Ray went in to shower first. The sky was gray, but the winds were pushing any rain clouds out to sea. My *aukane*, or spirit animal, was the porpoise, and I had been on surfboards since I was a baby. Right then, I wished that we could just grab a couple of boards and let the ocean wash away all the pain and sadness of the morning. But that was not to be.

A steady stream of traffic crawled along the Farrington Highway. Tourists in rented convertibles with the top down despite the gloomy weather. Farm trucks loaded with fertilizer and equipment. A barefoot twenty-something haole woman in a one-piece bathing suit walked past, her head tilted at an angle, as if it was too much trouble to hold it up straight.

The air usually smells fresh after a rainstorm, but out there all I could smell was automobile exhaust and a harsh wash of salt.

"You see those babies?" Mike asked, as we waited beside the motel office.

"Uh-huh. They looked like they were the same age, so they must have been twins. Just like Addie and Owen."

"Hit me kind of hard," Mike said. "Seeing them like that."

I looked down. I had few secrets from Mike; we had explored every inch of each other's body, and every corner of each other's psyche, in the years we had been together. "I cried."

He nodded. "Me, too."

Ray came out of the room in his pale green scrubs. "It's all yours," he said.

Mike and I went in together, though we showered separately. The stall was too small for both of us, and we weren't there for fun. We packed up our clothes for decontamination and put on the scrubs.

By the time we got out, Ray had already ordered sub sandwiches and bottles of water delivered for us from a local place, and the three of us sat around a picnic table and ate. It was funny to see Ray in the scrubs, when for our years at HPD, we'd worn aloha shirts and khakis, upgrading our wardrobes to dark slacks and white shirts to fit in at the Bureau. We'd both steadfastly refused to wear ties.

The EMT bus passed by on the way back from a call and returned us to where we'd parked. Ray's SUV and Mike's truck were the only vehicles left, besides a single HPD cruiser guarding the site.

I said goodbye to Mike, who was going to his office at the fire department headquarters in downtown Honolulu. Ray drove us to my house, where I changed into something resembling Bureau-approved attire, and then we went to his apartment, where he did the same. It was late afternoon by the time we returned to Kapolei and checked in with Salinas.

He had little to share from the work of the other agents. "We've got some evidence from the scene," I said. "Boat registration, Juki Net cards. We'll give them to the translation specialist. It looks like the people on the sailboat were headed for Seattle, so we'll have to look through the log and see how they ended up here."

"I spoke to the admiral in charge of the Coast Guard base," Salinas said. "He was able to confirm the box they took off the boat contains radioactive plutonium. He sent it to DC for further analysis, and he's put out feelers to see if it matches anything that could have gone missing from the Fukushima Dai-Ichi plant."

"From my experience with the ME's office, I can tell you they have a lot of chemical tests they can run on the bodies from the boat, but those all take time," I said.

"Keep me informed," he said, and then saw another agent and hurried away.

Ray and I went back to our office. I photocopied the boat registration and the Juki Net cards, and then looked up the translation specialist, Emily Sukihara, to see where I could find her. I was struck by her resemblance to Chikako Griffin—same oval face and black hair, though hers was cut in a shorter bob.

I knocked on the frame of her cubicle and said hello. "Can you read this?" I asked, showing her the paperwork.

She looked at the pages and nodded. "I'll get a translation together."

By the time I got back to the office Ray had pulled up a criminal record for Dale Griffin. "Used to live here, up to a couple of years ago," he said. "Last known place of work was this sunset-cruise place out of Ala Wai. Then he got pulled in for conspiracy to commit burglary. The way the complaint read, he'd call an accomplice with information on hotel guests, and then the accomplice broke into the rooms while the people were away."

"Away on a sunset cruise?"

"Wouldn't surprise me," Ray said.

In law, the difference between robbery and burglary is the presence of the victim. Steal something from me personally, that's robbery. Steal it from my house when I'm not there, that's burglary.

"Who was the accomplice?" I asked.

"Hank Owens, street name Weasel. Record for breaking and entering that stretches from here to Halawa, which not coincidentally was his latest address."

The Halawa Correctional Facility was a medium-security facility housing convicted felons, in the middle of the island. "From what I could piece together from Weasel's record," Ray continued, as we watched the captain give his spiel, "he was breaking into unoccupied boats, around the time Griffin was working here. After Griffin left the island, Weasel went back to his boat burglary gig, and a judge got fed up and sentenced him to do some real time. It looks like he pissed off one of the hard-core guys, who cut him with a homemade weapon."

"So he's a dead lead," I said.

"In a manner of speaking."

"Anything on the wife?"

He shook his head. "Chikako is clean."

The Sunset Ali'i, the boat Dale had worked on, would be leaving port in about an hour—just enough time for us to get there and interview the crew before they left. Ray and I drove in separate cars so we could go home when we were finished, and all the way down the H1 toward downtown I kept thinking about those two little babies. What had driven their parents to take them on such a long, dangerous ocean voyage?

I pulled into the parking lot at Ala Wai Yacht Harbor, where Gilligan and crew had left for their three-hour tour so many years before, with Ray right behind me. We followed the signs to the Sunset Ali'i, a catamaran painted in shades of red, orange and yellow. A big blond guy wearing a T-shirt that read "Kiss the Captain" was standing at the dock, shilling for customers.

"Detective Kanapa'aka, HPD," I said, showing him my badge. "You know a guy named Dale Griffin?"

"Dale? Sure. Used to work for me maybe two, three years ago."

"What happened to him after that?"

"He met this pretty little Japanese girl, tourist, on one of our cruises. They spent the rest of her vacation together, then a few months later he picked up and left for Japan."

"He ever get in trouble?" Ray asked.

The captain's eyes shifted toward a sunburnt middle-aged couple in matching aloha outfits: blue hibiscus on a shirt for him, red on a muumuu for her. "Gimme a minute," he said, and he walked over to them.

"Convenient time for him to ditch us," I said to Ray. The captain took some cash offered by the sunburnt couple then he helped them onto the boat, where his mate took charge of them.

"Sorry," he said, when he returned to us. "Gotta make a living, you know."

"How'd Griffin's burglary operation work?" Ray asked. "He'd get friendly with rich-looking passengers, find out where they were staying, then phone a friend?"

"I canned him as soon as I heard about the first complaint," the captain said. "He's a good guy at heart, Dale. Just gets caught up with bad people sometimes. I should have known something the first time I saw that Weasel guy hanging around." He sighed. "I didn't know Dale was back in town. What did he do now?"

"He just got in yesterday," I said. "DOA."

"He's dead?" The captain didn't look too surprised, or too upset either. "What happened to him?"

"That's what we're trying to figure out. He a good sailor?"

"Pretty good. Had his captain's license from somewhere back east. He was just bumming here, looking for a gig, when he worked for me." He nodded back to the catamaran. "This job's more about people skills than sailing. Dale could talk to most anybody, especially if he had a beer in his hand."

"You know anybody else he might have kept in touch with?" I asked.

He shook his head. "Hard to keep crew around here. They flake off or take off. Must have been through three or four mates since he left."

We thanked him and walked back toward our cars. "Any ideas?" I asked Ray.

"Go home, have dinner, play with my kid, go to bed, play with my wife, wake up tomorrow and start all over again."

4 – Special Delivery

Mike was already at home by the time I got there, and I could smell the charcoal on the backyard grill from the driveway. When I opened the front door Roby romped out, his golden tail waving.

"Hey, boy," I said, reaching down to ruffle behind his ears. Before I could get much scratching in, he had already taken off for the palm tree at the edge of the street, where he lifted his leg.

I followed him back into the house and out to the backyard as Roby rushed over to where Mike stood by the grill.

"How are you feeling?" Mike asked me. "No adverse effects from the radiation?"

"Unless being tired is one of them." I leaned up to kiss his cheek.

"I've got burgers ready to go. Take another shower, just to be safe, and then come back."

I followed Mike's instructions, then pulled on a pair of drawstring board shorts and rubber slippers. The burgers smelled *ono* – Hawaiian for delicious. He had already set the picnic table under the spreading kiawe tree.

Mike handed me a plate with a perfectly charred burger on it. " your case going?" he asked.

As I layered lettuce, tomato, mayo and ketchup on the burger, I told him about Dale Griffin's arrest record, and the conversation with the sailboat captain. "Not much to go on yet," I said. "We have to wait for information to come in from Japan, and then get it translated. And it's going to take a while for all the chemical tests, too."

We ate together in the shade, a light breeze blowing up from the Pacific, and it was so lovely there that it was hard to believe we'd spent the morning at such a gruesome location.

We carried the dirty dishes into the kitchen. "I probably need to learn more about radioactive materials," I said. "You think you can give me some background on this plant in Japan and what kind of materials they had on hand?"

"Let's go online and see what we can find out."

While I put the dishes in the dishwasher, Mike opened his laptop on the kitchen table. The house had been his before I moved in, and since neither of us were that into decorating we hadn't done much to change it. He'd framed a bunch of placemats and menus from Italian and Korean restaurants and hung them around the room, a visual statement about his ethnic heritage, and sometimes I'd look up and see a cartoon of the Leaning Tower of Pisa hung right next to an illustrated recipe for *bulgogi*, Korean-style marinated beef. Since I'd grown up in multi-ethnic Hawai'i, it didn't seem odd at all, but some people who came to our house were baffled.

I finished the dishes and joined Mike at the table. "This is interesting," he said, pointing at the screen. "The Unit 3 reactor the Fukushima plant used mixed oxide fuel which contained a small percentage of plutonium oxide as well as uranium oxide."

"Why is that interesting?"

"Because ordinary uranium isn't that toxic. You can carry a couple of grams of it around in your back pocket without feeling any effects."

I must have still looked confused, because he continued, "Plutonium, on the other hand, is highly toxic, especially when inhaled. And when you expose plutonium to moist air, it forms oxides and hydrides that can flake off. I heard that the box was damaged somehow, which would have exposed the plutonium to the atmosphere."

"Which would have been pretty moist in the middle of the Pacific, and the enclosed cabin would have heightened their exposure, right?"

He shrugged. "I'm no chemist. But you have four dead people, and that explanation makes sense."

"Can you use that plutonium to make a bomb?" I asked.

"You betcha," he said.

I sat back in my chair. "The Griffins didn't look like international terrorists," I said. "What were they doing with it? Were they just mules?"

"You can't FedEx a box of plutonium," Mike said. "Shipping companies do a basic scan of everything that goes through their warehouses. They'd pick up the radioactive signature, even if the box wasn't damaged, and they'd refuse to carry it."

"But boats wouldn't go through the same scrutiny," I said. "Especially one run by a family with little kids."

"And if the box hadn't gotten damaged, they could have completed their crossing and made their delivery."

I wondered if whoever they'd been planning to meet in Seattle knew that they'd run into trouble. Had Griffin been able to contact them and let them know he was aiming for Honolulu? Would someone be coming to Hawai'i in search of what was in that box? Who were they, and how could Ray and I find them?

Roby started clamoring for his evening walk, so Mike and I took him out into the gathering twilight. Two boys were tossing a ball back and forth, and down the street a neighbor was watering his flowerbeds. It was a peaceful evening in suburbia, a story being repeated on thousands of streets around the country. Ours was different only in the presence of white kukui blossoms on the trees; the yellow ilima flowers like tiny hibiscus, very popular in leis; and the lokelani, or pink rose, which my mother had been named for.

But appearances could be deceiving. A nice, normal-looking family had sailed into the islands, a common enough occurrence. But this boat had carried a deadly cargo, one that had killed everyone on board.

After we returned from our I walk, I checked my personal email. Mostly junk—our refrigerator manufacturer reminding us it was time to change the water filter; coupons from a local restaurant chain, and a sale on pooper scoopers at the pet store. I deleted most of it, saving only a newsletter from an author whose books I liked; a surfing video from my friend Harry, reminding me that we hadn't been out on the waves together for a long time; and an email from my mother with details of her latest genealogy project.

After my father passed away, she was at loose ends for a while. She remained in the condo they'd bought in Waikiki, driving to babysit her grandchildren now and then, but I could tell she'd been lonely. She had joined an online club for people interested in tracing their ancestors and was industriously working on our family tree. The Hawaiian side—from her mother and my dad's father—was pretty easy, because we'd had to prove Hawaiian descent years before for various state benefits. Her father had been born in Japan, and she'd traced him back to Shiogama Prefecture, where his family had been farmers for generations.

Lately she had been working on my father's mother and her family. My gran was born to Mormon parents in Idaho and the Mormons were great at gathering family records. She was excited that she'd found a couple of first cousins of my dad's still alive in Boise and Idaho Falls.

I read in our bedroom, and Mike watched TV downstairs. Just before ten, I joined him in the living room for the KVOL news. Lui had been working there since college, and had been promoted to station manager a few years before. Because of his connection, it was our channel of choice, though sometimes I got fed up with their "Exploding News All The Time" motto, accompanied by a graphic of lava flows.

Halfway through the broadcast, after reports from a deadly fire in Canada, a tsunami in Indonesia, and a revolt in one of the Russian satellite states, the perky female anchor said, "And now to Ralph Kim, following a story of a deadly sailboat crash on the Leeward Coast," and the scene shifted to a shot of the Usagi Maru.

Ralph Kim was an investigative reporter with the station, and I'd tangled with him a few times, first over my initial coming out as a gay cop. Since then, though, I'd run into him occasionally, often when

Lui sent him to try and get the inside scoop on a case.

From the position of the sun, it looked like Ralph's segment had been shot late in the day, long after Mike, Ray and I had left the scene. "I'm here at Ohikilolo Beach Park on the Leeward Coast, where police have quarantined the site of a sailboat crash which resulted in the death of a young couple and their infant children," he said, motioning behind him. "Police and Coast Guard sources refused to comment, but as you can see the site has been isolated with crime scene tape and hazardous materials warnings."

"Ralph, do you know why the site has been quarantined?" the anchor asked him.

"I spoke with an expert in infectious diseases at the University of Hawai'i earlier today," he said. "There are a number of airborne viruses which could have caused the family's deaths but he was unable to speculate about which kind could be involved here because of the lack of information."

The camera went back to the anchor. "Worrying news about a possible contagion on the Leeward Coast. We'll keep an eye on this developing story." She thanked Ralph and then went on to the next story.

"Typical KVOL," Mike said. "Milk an event for anything they can guess at."

"At least they don't know the real story," I said. "Though I'm sure they'll figure it out soon enough."

5 – *Log Lines*

The next morning work began with a status meeting convened by Francisco Salinas, looking spiffy as ever in his starched white shirt and slickly creased black slacks. "The press has already gotten hold of the story, though right now they're barking up the wrong tree." He looked at Ray and me. "Just to reiterate our policies here, any media inquiries go directly to Randy Vernon. We don't make any comments either on or off the record."

I squirmed in my seat. Salinas knew of my brother's connection to KVOL, and he had probably guessed I'd provided off-the-record information to Lui in the past. This was a clear signal there would be none of that on this case.

Emily Sukihara stepped to the laptop at the podium, hit a couple of keys, and a map of Japan appeared on the screen behind her. "The Juki Net cards indicate that Dale and Chikako Griffin lived in Hakodate, the third largest city on the island of Hokkaido, at the island's southern tip. The boat was registered there as well."

She clicked the mouse and a mug shot photo of Dale Griffin appeared. "This is the man found on the boat, Dale Griffin, born in Oceanside, California in 1985. After graduating from high school he got his captain's license from the Maritime Institute in San Diego. He was arrested several times in California for drug-related offenses but never convicted. He relocated to Honolulu in 2009, where he was arrested for conspiracy to commit burglary, but the charges were dropped. He moved to Japan early last year and married Chikako Kameda, a Japanese native."

Griffin's shaggy blond hair made him look like a good-natured surfer dude. He was unshaven in the photo, and I could make out a tattoo on his left bicep. Sukihara pointed and zoomed. "The tattoo there is his wife's name."

Sukihara clicked again to a candid photo of Chikako. "Chikako Kameda Griffin was born in Hakodate on Hokkaido in 1987. She graduated from Hokkaido University with a degree in English. Japanese citizen with no criminal record. One visit to the U.S. in 2010."

She stepped down and her place was taken by Special Agent Ryan Tomlinson, an African-American guy from Southern California who spoke in the cadences of the San Fernando Valley. "Working our way through known terrorist cells on the island," he said. "So far no connections."

That was it. He sat down. Ray nudged me, and I stood up and walked to the podium. "Ray and I did a thorough inspection of the boat yesterday. We ran background checks on the two adults and started an investigation into Griffin's background with an interview with his former employer. He mentioned Griffin's arrest and an accomplice, who died in prison about a year ago. No other known associates. He indicated that Griffin met his wife on the trip Emily mentioned, and moved to Japan soon after."

Out of the corner of my eye I saw that Salinas was making a note.

"The boat's original destination was Seattle, but something must have happened during the trip to take them off course. The ship's log has been decontaminated, so Ray and I will read through it today and continue to track both Griffins and look for any additional contacts. Autopsy results on the Griffins are expected today, which should confirm exposure to plutonium."

"Good job," Salinas said. He told the agent who coordinated with the Japanese to ask their police service about the Griffins. I waited at the podium for a beat, but when there were no questions I sat back down.

"You all know what to do," Salinas said. "We'll meet again tomorrow morning."

As Ray and I walked back to the office, my cell phone rang with a call from the Medical Examiner's office.

"All four victims had significant concentrations of plutonium in the lungs and the liver," Doc Takayama said. "Cause of death, acute organ failure. Method of death exposure to toxic levels of plutonium. This is a case I might want to write up for a medical journal. Not your everyday knife or gunshot wounds."

"Thanks, Doc," I said. That jived with what Mike and I had discussed the night before. As we sat down at our desks, I filled Ray in with what I'd learned. "But I don't know how you could steal plutonium if it's toxic."

"I can do some research on that," Ray offered.

"All right. And I'll look at the log and see if there are any clues there."

He went online, and I went down the hall to the evidence room, where I had to get an agent to unlock the cage and find the Usagi Maru's log for me. Someone had placed a sticker with the radioactive symbol on the plastic bag and for a moment I didn't want to touch it, even though I'd already handled the log, and the bag.

I used the marker hanging on a string at the door to the locker to sign my name and add the date and time. I was still nervous about contamination, but Mike had said the material we took off the boat was safe, and I believed him.

After all, I trusted him with my life every time we had sex without a condom— trusted that he was faithful to me, that he hadn't exposed himself to STDs, that he loved me and would never do anything to harm me.

I took the bag and carried it back to my desk. Though everyone in my family loved the ocean, we had never owned a boat of any kind, because my father often said a boat was a hole in the water you threw money into. Instead, our garage was crowded with surfboards, wakeboards, and pool floats.

I was curious to read Dale Griffin's log and see what boat ownership was really like. It was an oversized book in fake leather, with a stylized compass on the cover and the words YACHT LOG above it. The left-hand pages were headed "Log of the Yacht" with *Usagi Maru* penned in on the line beside it, followed by a space for day of the week and date. Beneath it were columns for *Time, Position, Course, Current, Wind* and *Weather*.

The right-hand pages were headed *Passage From* with a line, and beneath it were columns for *Engine or Sail* and *Comments*. At the very bottom of the page Griffin could record fuel and water taken on.

The first page was dated about a year before the Usagi Maru's departure from Hakodate. In the comments section, Griffin wrote about the purchase of the boat from one of Chikako's cousins, and all the work he had to put in to make it seaworthy. The Usagi Maru's maiden voyage was a trip across Uchiura Bay to the town of Muroran. It took six hours by sail—about sixty-four nautical miles at an average speed of about ten knots.

What seemed odd was that they left port at five in the evening, landing in Muroran at eleven, then after only a brief stop turned around and returned to Hakodate at six in the morning. I turned to my computer and looked up sunrise and sunset times and figured out that they'd left after dark and returned before sunrise. Why make a short trip like that in the dead of night?

The implication was that it wasn't a voyage they wanted to report to the authorities. And in the comments he said nothing about where they were going or what they were doing out so late.

> *Once we passed the lights of Hakodate, Chikako and I stood on the deck and looked at the stars. She picked out the three stars of Orion's belt, and right behind it was Canis Major with Sirius, the brightest star in the sky. She calls that constellation o-ee-nu, the big dog. It reminds me that no matter how different we are, we have so much in common.*

The comments on the following pages were equally chatty, with lots of information about Chikako and her pregnancy, and later how the twins, Tammy and Timmy, were acclimating to sea life. I got a real sense of his voice, and the way he must have charmed customers on those sunset cruises.

A month later, there was a trip through the Tsugaru Straits, also done at night, to the city of Aomori on the island of Honshu. According to Dale's comments, they delivered a package to some cousins of Chikako's, and then spent a few days socializing with family. From Aomori they made several short trips around the northern tip of the island and down along the Pacific coast. I plowed forward because I didn't know what would turn out to be important, but my attention perked up as the Usagi Maru began a trip down the shore of Honshu.

Dale seemed to be able to speak basic Japanese, like me, and had very little knowledge of the written language, though he could manage the common nautical signs. One entry made me curious.

> *Passing by all these little towns along the coast, like the ones that were washed away. Breaks my heart to think of all the death and damage. If it was up to me I'd have turned back miles ago.*

I sat up and stretched, my back kinking up after hunching over the loopy handwriting. If it was up to him, he'd have turned back. Were they on some kind of humanitarian mission? Maybe they were going to rescue members of Chikako's family who'd been made homeless by the tsunami.

Somehow I doubted that.

I continued to read. The farthest south they got was the town of Shiogama, on Matsushima Bay. They anchored offshore of one of the islands for several days.

> *While we wait, doing more maintenance. Repaired a tear in the staysail, polished the teak on the bow. Built two cribs into the V-berth for the babies, keep them safe if the water gets rough.*

What were they waiting for, I wondered? Without stating a reason for the delay, Dale indicated that they were under way again. The following days were filled with notes about the boat and the return trip to Hakodate, with almost no personal information.

They remained there for forty-eight hours, provisioning for a long trip. Dale took an inventory of everything from cloth diapers to powdered milk to energy bars. He calculated the distance to Seattle and made notes about the kind of weather they could expect. They envisioned a voyage of 40-50 days, though they provisioned for an extra week.

Never once did he mention why they were embarking on such a long, dangerous trip. The first log entry of their trans-Pacific trip began with a weather report.

> *Morning started warm and sunny. Slow going out of Hakodate until we jibed around the corner of Cape Shiriyazaki. Listened for the coordinates of the Kuroshio and caught it a few miles off shore. Started really moving, doing 7 knots through the water but 11 over the bottom thanks to the current.*

I stopped to look up the Kuroshio, which I discovered was also called the Black Stream. Like the Gulf Stream in the Atlantic, it brought warm tropical water north.

> *At dusk the wind died. Only motion came from the Kuroshio. Set the wind vane and slept til sunrise when the wind picked up, battling against the current. Tough sailing, beating into the wind, making 6.2 knots.*

Dale was a steady logger. Every day he recorded the GPS readings, the wind speed and how fast they were moving. Chikako was sad about leaving Japan, but interested to spend some time in the U.S. Dale made a few guarded references to bringing in some serious money in the near future, which he planned to use to buy a house for his family and set up his own charter business.

Though he never said anything about his dangerous cargo, that had to be the source of the money. He was going to get paid well for making this delivery. But who was paying? And what were they going to use the plutonium for?

The answers to those questions didn't seem to be in the log. There was a lot of technical stuff about sails and waves and wind speed that I skimmed over, until the Griffins hit a storm. Dale's entries became hurried, his handwriting worse. He recorded wind speed and bits of damage to the boat—water seeping in, the bilge pump jamming, and so on.

> *Staysail tore and had to take it down. Chikako did*

the sewing while I navigated. Got the staysail back up and continued riding the current.

Waves are fucking ferocious—all nasty churning gray, streaked with white foam, maybe 10 to 15 feet high. Babies crying below, so Chikako too busy to help. Tethered to the jackstay, crawled on hands and knees up to the foredeck in 40-knot winds. Up there it was like swimming, with all the water coming over the bow. Managed to get sails secured and crawled back to the cockpit. Waves pack a real wallop out there, and the spray stings like razor blades on your skin. Cold, wet snow and slush and 30-40 ft waves washing across the deck with no place to hide above, and no heater down below.

Crashed in bed in wet clothes, trying to dry them by body heat while Chikako took the helm. Woke up and like magic, storm was gone and skies were sunny and the wind was high. Pod of Pacific white-sided dolphins streaked past; babies really love them.

Took inventory of all the damage. Lightning hit the VHF antenna and fried the radio. Cargo knocked loose, case banged up. Chikako freaking but I can't. She wants to drop it overboard and head home. Think it's too late for that but can't tell her.

They hit a couple of days of good weather, and Dale had a chance to fix everything that had broken, except the radio, which was unusable. The storm had knocked them off course, and Dale had to do a lot of calculations using GPS and longitude and latitude. Most of it made no sense to me; I was accustomed to being able to call up my location on my phone or computer and get a clear map of where I was.

I knew someone who could help me, though, and I called my friend Terri's husband. Terri had been my best gal pal all through my years at Punahou, the elite private school in Honolulu my brothers and I had been fortunate to attend. We had remained close, weathering numerous personal storms together, and I was pleased that she'd finally recovered from the death of her first husband and had remarried, a few years before.

Levi Hirsch had been a corporate mogul in Seattle, then ditched it all to gunkhole around the islands in his sailboat. When I called him he said he'd be glad to meet me for lunch and explain the nautical stuff to me.

I photocopied the relevant pages and then went back to read further. My eyes were glazed over until I read what he'd written about his babies.

> *First Tammy wouldn't eat. Then Timmy. Both of them pale, dehydrated.*

I knew what was coming and I wasn't ready to face it. I was glad to have the excuse of leaving the office to meet Levi.

6 – Ohana

When I pulled up at the Hawksbill Bar, Levi was leaning against his BMW convertible talking on his cell phone. He was a good-looking guy in his late forties, a few years older than Terri and I. His black hair was wavy and flecked with silver, and I noticed as I got out of my Jeep that it looked like he'd put on weight.

He ended his call and we hugged hello. We took a booth near the front door and both ordered cheeseburgers and the Waialua root beer they had on tap. "Don't tell Terri about this," he said. "She's got me on a healthy diet and it's killing me."

So I was right about the weight gain. "Pinky swear," I said, putting up my hand.

Levi laughed, and matched my gesture. "Haven't done that since I was a kid."

"Dakota picked it up somewhere," I said, as the server returned with our drinks. I experienced a momentary pang, missing the kid, even though he was on the same island with us and we saw him at least once or twice a month.

Levi picked up his mug and sipped, then said, "Before we get distracted, tell me what you need to talk about."

I put a manila folder containing photocopies of the Usagi Maru's log on the table, a slab of wood covered with nautical maps and a heavy sheen of lacquer. "This is the log from the sailboat that crashed," I said. "I thought you as a sailor might have some insights."

I turned the folder so that it faced him and he flipped it open. He sipped his root beer as he scanned through the first couple of pages, stopping when he got to Griffin's plans for the trans-Pacific trip. "So they started out with the Black Stream," he said. "Makes sense. You know why they call it that?"

I shook my head.

"Because the water's a deep blue, almost black. Dangerous. The Kuroshio also impacts the weather, particularly in the early spring, which is when these people were traveling. Low pressure systems—you know, rain and wind—start there and move northeast towards the Bering Sea and Alaska. Because the current is so strong, these winds can raise steep waves—which would be dangerous for a boat of this size."

He looked back at the log and traced his finger. "Fortunately, this guy seems like a pretty savvy sailor, and he usually managed to find the balance between riding the current and working with the wind. He's also smart enough to know about great circle navigation."

"And what's that?" I asked.

"A great circle is the shortest distance between two points on the surface of a sphere. The earth isn't spherical, but it's close enough for navigation purposes. This guy followed the route pretty closely—except here." He pointed at the entry I'd noticed about the big storm that had damaged the boat. "This is where he decides to switch course from Seattle to Honolulu."

The server brought our burgers, and we pushed aside the log to protect it. "How are the keikis?" he asked, using the island term for little kids.

"We're actually able to have conversations with them," I said. "Complete sentences. Addie loves her crayons and she can name at least a dozen of the colors. Owen is fearless on his tricycle though I freak out every time I think he's going to fall over."

He laughed. "The worrying never stops, you know. Ilana is twenty-four and Susan is twenty-two, and I still worry about them all the time, especially Ilana in Israel. She lives in Haifa and works for a high-tech company—she's far from the border, but every time I hear about a restaurant getting bombed or a knife attack, I have to check in with her. Susan's in her last year of medical school, and every couple of weeks she calls me up crying about how exhausted she is."

I did some quick math. "You were, what, twenty-two when Ilana was born? Weren't you still in grad school then?"

He nodded. "I had just started my MBA at Harvard. Fortunately Jenny's family had plenty of money, so that made things easier. We were the only grad students we knew who had a nanny. But it was still hard reading and writing case studies and cramming for exams with a baby crying. Susan was born right after I graduated. I got a job on Wall Street and we moved to Manhattan. I was pretty much an absentee dad—working long hours, helping small tech companies go public. When one of them offered me a job as the CFO, we thought it would be a chance to change things up. We moved to Seattle but I was still on the road, only this time flying east instead of west."

He shrugged. "That's a big part of the reason why Jenny and I divorced. I just wasn't there." He reached for his burger. "Don't make that mistake with your kids, Kimo. Or with Mike."

"My dad worked long hours too," I said, between bites. "But he taught me to surf, and every Saturday we'd go down to Waikiki. Sometimes he'd stay, sometimes he'd have a job to finish. But I knew that my brothers and I were always his priority."

"I'd say you all turned out pretty well as a result," he said. "I got lucky with my girls. I'm trying to do a better job with Danny."

Terri's son Danny was fifteen, and it had been ten years since his father, a Honolulu cop, had been murdered. It had taken him and his mother a long time to recover, and Mike and I had spent a lot of time with him as favorite uncles. We hadn't all been together in a while. "We should get together soon," I said. "Have a big luau."

"Sounds good. But let's wait until Terri has me off this diet. I want to be able to eat my fill of your mother's kalua pork."

Terri wasn't going to let up if he kept sneaking cheeseburgers, but I didn't say anything. We finished our food and after the server took away the dirty dishes we went back to the log.

"You said the storm threw them off course," I said. "Why would Griffin aim for Honolulu instead of continuing to Seattle?"

I moved across the table to sit next to him so we could read the log together, and Levi pointed to the place in the log where the staysail had torn, and the waves had been "fucking ferocious."

"You can see him recalculating his coordinates here. But it takes them a while to repair everything. And he's staying south to avoid more storms. Then here, they cross the International Dateline which separates the Eastern and Western Hemispheres. At this point, the closest port of call is Honolulu. It looks like he's planning to head to Ala Wai, repair the boat, and then take off for Seattle."

"We pulled a box off the boat with hazard warnings on it, and it looked like one corner of it had been smashed in. The box got damaged in that storm, and that let the radiation out into the boat."

"Well, that sucks," Levi said. We went through the rest of the log together. The last log entry was almost impossible to read because Dale Griffin's handwriting was so weak.

> *Set the wind vane for O'ahu. Going to lie down beside Chikako, and hope we make landfall in time to get help.*

Neither Levi or I said anything more.

When I got back to Kapolei, I found Ray on the phone. "All right, thank you," he said. "I'll keep you informed on this end."

When he hung up he said, "That was the legat in Tokyo, Jutta Dore."

For a moment I thought Ray was speaking French. "Excuse me? You love me?"

Ray looked at me like I'd lost my mind. "What are you talking about?"

"*Je t'adore,*" I said. "In French it means I love you."

"Sorry, I studied Italian in school. This guy's name is Jutta Dore." He spelled it for me. "Emily Sukihara gave me his name and suggested we coordinate with him."

Though the FBI tracked domestic crime, as opposed to the CIA, the Bureau maintained offices in many overseas locations, called legal attaches, or legats. There were over sixty legats around the globe, tasked with building relationships with local law enforcement and intelligence and security services.

"He says there was a lot of chaos in the days right after the tsunami hit, so it's hard to get clear records on who had access to the Unit Three reactor, the only one that used plutonium. He's continuing to dig, though." He sat back in his chair. "While I was talking to him, I started to wonder how a low-life like Dale Griffin, an American in Japan, could have the connections to score a transportation gig like this. And I thought of Julie's cousin Salvatore."

"He lives in Japan?"

Ray shook his head. "No, he's a small time hoodlum back in Philly. When I wanted to know about mob stuff I went to him. I'm thinking maybe Chikako had a cousin like Sal, and he hooked Dale up with this trip. So I asked Dore to do some research on Chikako's family, see if she had any shady connections."

"Good idea." I opened the log book and flipped to the page where the Usagi Maru had been heading south after the tsunami. "Here's what I've been working on."

I pulled up a map site on my computer and turned the screen to face Ray. "Dale and Chikako stayed here for a couple of days. Shiogama, in Miyagi Prefecture." I hit the button for directions. "It's only about an hour and a half from Fukushima, and it looks like the closest big port that's outside of the quarantine region. The Japanese equivalent of Julie's cousin could have brought the box of plutonium to them while they were in port."

"It makes sense," Ray said, as he read the log entries. "They leave Shiogama and go back to Hakodate. Stay there just a couple of days then head for open ocean. That sounds like they've gotten their marching orders."

I flipped ahead a couple of pages in the log book. "I wanted to ask you something," I said, when I reached the place where Chikako had suggested Dale throw the damaged box overboard. I pointed to it. "He says here it's too late to get rid of the cargo. What do you make of that?"

He read the entries, then looked up. "Could be a couple of things. Maybe he knows the radiation has already escaped, and dumping the box wouldn't help."

"I don't think so," I said. "He's no expert on radiation. I bet he didn't even know exactly what was in that box."

"Maybe he means it's too late moneywise," Ray suggested. "That he's already accepted a payment for the delivery, and doesn't have the cash to pay it back."

"And he'd be on the hook for the value of the cargo, too," I said. "I mean, he's just the delivery boy, right? If he tosses the box, he'll have to pay whoever hired him its value."

Ray nodded. "Which he and Chikako sure couldn't afford."

"Especially if they were hooked up with somebody like Julie's cousin Sal, with Japanese mafia connections."

"Definitely wouldn't want to piss off somebody like that."

Ray and I read the last few entries in the log together. Griffin's handwriting got weaker as he realized that whatever had made the babies sick was working on him and Chikako as well. I could sense a desperation in his desire to make better time toward O'ahu.

> *Tammy went first. Timmy was a little fighter, though he only held out for a few more hours. After she put them into their cribs, Chikako went to bed and wouldn't get up. Kept pushing the Usagi, hopping over the waves like the little rabbit she is. When Chikako got up, all she did was puke. Tried to get her to eat. Told her gotta stay strong for me, babe, but it didn't work.*

Ray pointed at that entry. "How far are they from O'ahu here?" he asked.

I did some quick calculations. "A couple of days, if they made good time. I wonder if Dale ever made the connection, that his babies were sleeping on top of nuclear waste."

"Chikako was pretty small, too," Ray said. "At least in comparison to her husband."

We looked back at the log. Chikako had hung on another week, though she wouldn't get out of bed and would only take small sips of water. Probably a combination of the radiation poisoning and the despair over the deaths of her babies.

I couldn't imagine what that must have been like. If anything happened to Addie or Owen, Mike was a certified EMT, his father a doctor, his mother a nurse. We had hospitals close by, and a whole ohana here to help us.

The Griffins had been stuck on a boat in the middle of the North Pacific, with no radio and no way to contact a ship anywhere in the area. How much harder had it been to watch their children die, not knowing why, not being able to help them or get them help. It didn't look like Dale had ever figured out what was causing the trouble, or I had to believe he'd have thrown the box overboard after the babies died, at least to save himself and his wife.

7 – Good Animals

I was staring at the log book again, trying to come up with new ideas, when my cell rang with an unknown number. As a cop, you can't ignore those calls; you never know when it could be a source or a suspect. "FBI, Detective Kanapa'aka," I said.

"Good afternoon, detective." I recognized the voice immediately—Ralph Kim, the investigative reporter KVOL. "A source told me you were out at the sailboat crash yesterday..." he began.

"You know the drill, Ralph," I said. "We can't talk to the press. If you have any questions about any Bureau operation, you contact our media coordinator. Name and number on the website."

"Come on, Kimo, we're old pals. Tell you what, I'll take anything you say off the record."

"First of all, I'd call our relationship more adversarial than old pals, Ralph. And you don't have to keep this off the record. The official word is no comment." I ended the call before he could argue any further.

"You know what's going to happen next," Ray said.

I looked up at him. "My brother Lui is going to call. He's going to ask me for a personal favor. He'll try to guilt me into giving him some information. Maybe remind me of all those times when our dad was too busy to take me surfing, and he took me instead."

Ray laughed. "And?"

"And I'll remind him of all the times he and Haoa told me that I was adopted. That I was a mistake, because I was so much younger than they were."

"Good to know you've got your family dynamics in order." He leaned back in his chair. "Any ideas on how we can figure out who Griffin was planning to turn the plutonium over to?"

"Some kind of terrorist group?"

"On U.S. soil," Ray said. "And you can't just hand over plutonium to your garden variety disaffected youth, right? Has to be someone with some knowledge of nuclear fission."

We plunged into FBI research on major groups that supported terror, from the anti-abortion groups to the white supremacists, with brief stops at animal rights activists. We found several different groups that counted among their members people with some science background which might include knowledge of nuclear weapons.

"Of course, you can find instructions on how to build a bomb online," Ray said. "So any lunkhead could believe that if he could just get the right stuff he could blow up the world."

"But even lunkheads have reasons why they do what they do," I said.

We had a mass of data that would take a skilled analyst days to sift through. We made a couple of faint attempts, searching for key words like plutonium in the files, but many of them consisted of scanned documents that weren't searchable automatically.

"What about if we narrow the field to the Pacific Northwest?" Ray asked. "Griffin was headed for Seattle originally."

"But whoever picked it up could have driven it anywhere. Remember, if the box hadn't been damaged it would have been safe to carry."

I hadn't touched my computer for a few minutes, and the power save feature kicked in and the screen went dark. I stared at my reflection, seeing my own Japanese heritage staring back at me. "Whoever was scheduled to pick up the plutonium had to have some kind of Japanese connection," I said.

"So we start with anyone in one of those groups who has Japanese heritage as well as a background in nuclear arms," Ray said.

We found a couple of possibilities, including a Nisei named Brian Kurokawa. He was born in Seattle to Japanese immigrant parents. His father was a professor of chemistry at the University of Washington, and Brian had been in veterinary school when he dropped out during his second year to become an animal activist. He had volunteered with PETA and Greenpeace, and then a few years before had founded his own organization, dedicated to stopping logging in the Pacific Northwest. He had been arrested a dozen or more times for trespassing, raids on forestry companies, and the destruction of private property.

"He'd have the science knowledge to build a bomb," Ray said. "Or he could find the information he needs online."

"But imagine the devastation," I said. "Think of all the little birds and bunnies that would die."

"Sometimes innocent animals have to die for the greater good," Ray said. "He could wipe out an area with a small bomb, then leave it to Mother Nature to rebuild. Look what's happening outside Chernobyl."

We'd both read an article a few weeks before about the resurgence of flora and fauna in the area around the shuttered nuclear reactor. Without humans there to tame the land, forests had begun to grow, and animals unchecked by human predation had thrived.

Ray began compiling a dossier on Kurokawa, and I kept looking. I found a couple of crazy guys like the Unabomber, well-educated men who had retreated to the woods and yet continued to issue manifestos telling the rest of us what was wrong with our world. A couple of them were located in the wilderness of Idaho, Oregon and Washington state, which put them close enough to Seattle to drive there and pick up a load of plutonium.

One guy who intrigued me was Art Duncan, a one-time employee of the Lawrence Livermore Labs in California who had taken early retirement because he disagreed with the government's policies. The group he had founded, the Nuclear Protection Organization, advocated the active use of nuclear weapons to subdue nations and non-governmental organizations that opposed the United States.

He and his wife Bethany had moved to a remote homestead in the Idaho panhandle, and begun attracting followers who shared his disdain of minorities and foreigners. They advocated English-only schools. Interestingly there was no religious component, though many of those who followed Duncan were Evangelical Christians.

By the time we left for the day, we had a list of vague possibilities, but nothing that specifically connected anyone to the Griffins' deadly cargo.

Mike got home early and fed and walked Roby, then met me for dinner at a small Italian restaurant a few blocks from the house. Vinyl booths, travel posters of Italy on the walls, and the soundtrack hadn't changed in decades—a rotating mix of Frank Sinatra, Dean Martin and Don Ho. But it was one of the few Italian restaurants Mike believed cooked as well as his Nonna, his father's mother.

We ordered the calamari appetizer to share, chicken marsala for him and piccata for me, and I told him about my lunch with Levi Hirsch. "He said we should all get together soon," I said.

"That would be great. We haven't done anything fun for a while."

"Hey, we've both been working," I said. "Without Dakota around it's easy to just stay in." It was true; when Dakota lived with us, we were always taking him places on the weekend, going to family parties so he could feel part of our ohana. With him out of the house we'd been relishing the quiet and the chance to just laze around and do nothing.

Under the music, Mike and I talked about our days, then dug into our dinners. By the time I finished my chicken, I was yawning.

"I'm not keeping you awake, am I?" Mike asked.

"Long day," I said. "Two long days in a row. I just want to go home and crash."

"Don't let me stop you," he said. "After all, we just had sex this morning, right? Got to have tired you out. That was the second time this month."

I kicked him under the table. "I didn't realize you were keeping track."

He leaned forward and said, in a low voice, "A man has needs, you know."

It made me laugh, but then I saw the look on his face. I pulled out my cell phone. "Let me see when I can fit you in."

"If you send me a meeting request for sex I'm going to take that phone and shove it…"

"Chill out," I said. "This is our life now. We have responsibilities." I scanned through my appointments. "We don't have anything scheduled this weekend, and guess what? Sunday is Valentine's Day." I raised my eyebrows. "I can pencil you in for sex on Saturday."

"In your case it is a pencil."

"Yeah, and I'll write all over your ass with it," I said. I left him to pay the check and drove home. Roby met me at the door, desperate to get outside for a pee, and immediately zoomed past me to the palm tree in the front yard, where he lifted his leg. Then the big goofy dog rushed back to me and jumped up on me. "Did the puppy miss me?" I asked as I ruffled behind his big floppy ears. "Did you miss your Papa K?"

Mike and I watched the late news on KVOL for any update on the sailboat story. This time Ralph Kim was outside the morgue, where he announced that the family on the Usagi Maru had died of radiation poisoning.

"The sailboat has been towed to an undisclosed location," he said in a serious voice. "There are concerns that the radiation may be endangering the Leeward Coast, but spokesmen for the FBI and the Honolulu PD both refused comment."

The camera switched back to the anchor. "That's worrying news, Ralph. You'll keep on top of this story for us?"

"Absolutely. The safety of our audience is very important to KVOL."

As long as they could get ratings from it.

8 – Breaks

The next morning as I was walking through the office parking lot I spotted the woman from Customs and ICE who had been in our first status meeting. "Morning," I said, reaching out to shake her hand. "We met the other day, I'm Kimo Kanapa'aka."

"From HPD," she said. "Claudia Jervis." Her grip was strong.

"What would the procedure have been if the Usagi Maru hadn't crashed?"

"The usual routine for an incoming yacht is to call the Harbormaster and check in, then dock. They have to go through formal clearance within forty-eight hours."

"Which means what, exactly?"

"Similar to what you'd do if you came in by plane. For yachts, Form 1303 is a Ships Stores Declaration. Who's on board, how long you're staying, what you're carrying. Form 1304 is the Crew's Effects Declaration—what each member of the crew is bringing into the country. Plus a copy of the outbound clearance form, also called a zarpe, from the previous port."

We came to the building's front door. "Nobody can go onshore except for the person reporting to Customs, who has to go back to the yacht until all the paperwork is finished. We're pretty serious about these rules. Penalties can be high, up to and including forfeiture of the yacht."

"Would anybody search the ship? Dogs sniffing for contraband, that kind of thing?"

"Not as a matter of course. If there was something suspicious,

-51-

sure. But if this guy had landed at Ala Wai with an American passport, a wife and two babies, and he had a convincing story about relocating back to the U.S., he'd probably have gotten a welcome and a couple of signatures."

When I got to the office I told Ray what I'd heard from Claudia Jervis. "It's a pretty good cover for transporting the plutonium," I said. "If that storm hadn't hit, they could have easily slipped past border controls in Seattle."

We both settled in at our computers, reading email and handling paperwork. At the sound of a rap against the doorframe, Ray and I both looked up.

"Got a minute?" Ryan Tomlinson asked. Tall and ebony-skinned, he was the agent from the High-Tech Intelligence Task Force.

"Sure. Welcome to our humble home," I said, motioning him to the visitor's chair between Ray's desk and mine.

"That sailboat case? Been looking at a guy who might be connected. A student at Honolulu Community College. Any contacts over there?"

I couldn't help it; from his surfer-dude accent and his slouch, I thought *Valley Boy*.

"What do you need?" I asked. "Addresses, class schedules?"

"We've got that. I'm looking for information on a guy named Bakir Al-Sarary, a Yemeni national with a student visa. He's studying environmental engineering and belongs to an Arab student club at HCC. He attends services at a mosque in Manoa we've had our eyes on for a while, because the imam there can get pretty strident."

"There must be other students who go to that mosque," I said.

"Yeah, but he's the only one who has an arrest record for brawling at protests. He's gotten fines and warnings and community service. Sounds like a loose cannon, and the kind of kid who could be recruited for something."

"I don't have the contacts at HCC I used to," I said. In the years after I first came out of the closet, I'd mentored a gay teen group in Waikiki, and some of those kids had gone on to college. But I'd had to give up volunteering once I transferred to the FBI and the kids I knew had graduated and joined the workforce.

"How about a company called Island Transport?" Tomlinson asked. "Al-Sarary has an internship there, which gives him access to the port of Honolulu."

Ray shook his head, and I said, "Not off the top of my head. I can ask around."

Tomlinson said he'd appreciate any help, and left. I pulled up the website for Island Transport, who handled transshipment between the harbors of Port Hawai'i and commercial locations within the islands. "I don't see the connection, though," I said to Ray. "Griffin didn't know he was heading to Honolulu until he hit that storm."

"And with his radio broken, he couldn't have communicated with anyone on land once his heading changed."

I sighed. "No stone unturned, though." I sat back and ran through my mental Rolodex. I'd never heard of the company before, so I doubted I knew anyone who worked there. But I did know an awful lot of people, and in the past I'd been able to find someone who knew someone.

I called Terri, who because of her family connections and her charitable work, had a whole network of contacts, but she didn't know anyone at Island Transport either. "Did you check with Harry?" she asked.

"He's next on my list."

Harry Ho had gone to Punahou with Terri and me, and his network was just as extensive as mine and Terri's. He was a tech wizard, consultant and entrepreneur, and tied closely to the Chinese community through his family and his church.

"Howzit, brah," I said, when he answered. "Got that surf video you sent. Very cool. You know anybody who works for a company called Island Transport?"

"Let me think." I knew he was doing the same thing I had, going through his list of contacts and their contacts. After a minute he said, "You know Nick Smart? Surfer?"

I had surfed almost every morning when I lived in Waikiki, but I'd scaled way back since moving to Aiea Heights and becoming a family man. "What break?" I asked, trying to establish where on the island the guy surfed.

"I run into him sometimes up on the North Shore," he said. "He owns a furniture company in Haleiwa."

Something clicked. "Haole guy?" I asked. "Forty-something, with shark fin tattoos on both arms?"

"That's him. The furniture he sells is manufactured in Indonesia, comes into the port. Maybe he'd know somebody at the transport company."

"Thanks, brah. That's a good lead."

When I Googled Nick Smart, I recognized his photo and learned that his company was called Unique Teak. I called the company's number and the receptionist said he wouldn't be in until two.

With that information, I knew where he was. Winter was the prime surf season on the North Shore, and I had a hunch that if I could find the best waves that morning, I'd find him. My surf report app indicated that due to the northwest swell, a break called Backyards could expect very fast, advanced waves with steep walls and thick lips.

I looked up at Ray. "Want to go for a ride?"

As we walked out to the parking lot I told him what I'd learned. "You think you can find him based on where the surf is strong?"

"It's where I'd be if I could."

We took the H1 to the interchange with the H2 and headed up into the center of the island, passing Schofield Barracks as we climbed. I put an old Keola Beamer CD in, and we listened to the mellow slack-key guitar as we drove. As the Kamehameha Highway crested over the Ko'olau, the North Shore was spread out before us, and we could see miles of rushing surf. Then we dipped down toward Haleiwa.

Every possible parking spot along the Kam was taken as we approached Backyards, a surf break halfway along the stretch between Sunset Point Beach and Kaunala Beach. A mix from junkers to expensive SUVs were parked nose-in, flat against the roadway or sideways against a screen of vegetation.

I pulled into a narrow spot with a yellow curb, and put my police decal on the dashboard. Then I stepped out of the Jeep and inhaled the salt air. The waves were crashing against the beach and the water was filled with guys and girls in neoprene rash guards, the form-fitting rubberized athletic shirts that protected surfers from encounters with sharp coral. They were mostly black or white, though there were a few bright colors thrown into the mix.

I could make out every kind of board from short thrusters, used in competition and shredding; fish, with wider, rounder noses, and swallow tails; all the way up to long, narrow guns and stable, looming longboards. I wanted to be out there with them so much it was like a physical ache in my stomach.

"You bring the screen shot of this guy?" Ray asked, bringing me back to the present.

I handed it to him. "He's about forty, buzz cut blond hair."

We scanned the incoming surfers. "There he is," I said, pointing to the right. "The white shirt with that red and blue print on the back." We watched as he rode the wave, turning on the lip to ride parallel to the shore for a moment, expertly avoiding a gremmie, or inexperienced surfer, wobbling on a long board. The wave jacked up and Smart shot down the green wall, cutting a foamy trail behind him. He slid gracefully to the shore after a couple of turns, and I walked toward him.

"Nick!" I called, and waved.

He shook the water from his head and looked our way. "Hey, Kimo, howzit?" he asked. I wasn't surprised that he recognized me, though we'd only spoken occasionally. I'd gotten a lot of publicity when I was dragged out of the closet, and again after I solved the murders of a couple of surfers.

"You were really charging out there," I said. "Wish I was on your side of the waves instead of this side."

I introduced Ray. "Got a minute for a question or two?"

As he planted his board in the sand, I recognized the wave design on the back of his rash guard, a copy of a Hokusai block print of a cresting wave over a full orange moon, with Mount Fuji silhouetted in the background. "About what?" he asked.

"You know anything about a company called Island Transport?"

"Sure. They bring all my furniture up from the port to my warehouse."

"You ever run across a college student there named Bakir Al-Sarary?"

Nick shook his head. "It's all computerized these days. I can log in from my phone and see the status of my shipments. Never have to talk to a human being. What's this about?"

"Just gathering information. Know anybody at all there we could talk to?"

"I do. I used to date a gal who worked there. She might be able to help you. Her name is Mindy Kerner."

He must have seen the look on my face because he asked, "You know her?"

"Let's just say she's a blast from the past. Haven't been in touch with her for years. Don't suppose you have her number, do you?"

"Sure. My phone's in my car. Right over there." He pointed toward a bright yellow Corvette.

He walked ahead of us, and Ray asked, "A blast from your past?"

"And not a particularly good one," I grumbled.

Ray knew that I had been conflicted about my sexuality when I was in my teens and twenties. I had slept with a lot of women, hoping each would be the one to quell the uncomfortable urges I had about men. It took a near-death experience for me to realize that those urges were never going to go away, and that if I wanted any kind of life I'd have to accept them.

Nick's car was right across from the break. "You must have gotten here early this morning to score such a prime spot," I said to

Nick when we reached him.

"I get up at six most days. Listen to the surf report, then go where the waves are."

He retrieved his cell from the car's glove compartment and read the number off, which I added to my own phone. "Mahalo, brah," I said. "Enjoy the waves."

"I plan to." He gave me a shaka, the two-fingered wave, which I returned, and he went back toward his board.

"So," Ray said, when he was gone. "This Mindy Kerner. Somebody you slept with?"

Ray was pretty cool when it came to sex talk. He had majored in sociology in college, taken courses in human sexuality, and had a gay cousin who had been his best friend as a kid. But we didn't share much about what we did in our respective bedrooms.

"Yeah. Short-term deal. Last time I saw her was a few months after I came out," I said. "We ran into each other at Ala Moana and I was surprised that she seemed real happy to see me."

"Who wouldn't be?" Ray asked.

I ignored him and started back toward the Jeep. "I was worried that she'd lash out at me about dating her when I was gay. But instead she invited me over to her apartment that night to talk about old times, and she wouldn't let me say no."

An HPD cruiser was pulled up beside my Jeep, the uniformed officer behind it, taking down my license number. "Give me a break," I muttered.

He looked about sixteen, and fresh out of the academy. "This your vehicle, sir?" he asked, as I approached, my keys in hand.

"We're on the job," I said, motioning to Ray with my head. "I'm going to pull out my wallet now." I slid it out slowly and opened it to my detective shield. "I did put the placard up on the windshield."

"Didn't get that far," he said. "You guys have a good day."

We thanked him and climbed into the Jeep. While I waited for the uniform to unblock us, I dialed the number Nick Smart had given me. "Mindy? It's Kimo Kanapa'aka," I said when she answered. I shifted the phone so that Ray could hear the conversation.

"I'm married," she said.

"Um. Congratulations. But I called in reference to an investigation."

I could hear the relief in her voice. Funny that she'd be relieved it was a police matter, not a personal one. "Oh, sure. What's up?"

"I understand you work for Island Transport?"

"I did, for a while. But the money sucked, so I went back to being a legal secretary last month."

The uniform pulled away, but I didn't want to drive while I was on the phone. Bad form, you know, considering it's illegal unless you have a Bluetooth, and I didn't want to waste time plugging mine in with Mindy on the line. "Did you know a guy there called Bakir Al-Sarary?" I asked.

"What a pain in the ass!" she said. "He's just an intern but he had to poke his nose into everything. He's in some kind of environmental safety program at HCC, and he wanted to know everything about the port, all the entrances and access codes, why the trucks took certain routes. He drove us all crazy."

I looked at Ray, and it looked like he had figured out what I had. An unusual interest in a vital node like the port of Honolulu was always a red flag.

"What happened?" Mindy asked. "Is Bakir in trouble?"

"We're just looking for information right now," I said. "Did he ever mention any friends to you, talk about his religion, anything personal?"

"He wasn't the kind of guy I wanted to be friends with," she said. "Real serious. I don't think anybody at work liked him."

"Mahalo, Mindy." Before I hung up, I had to indulge my curiosity. "Um. Did you end up marrying that guy Bobby?"

She laughed. "He was like five boyfriends ago, Kimo. Nope, I married a real nice guy, a real straight arrow. If you ever meet him…"

"Don't worry, I won't say a word," I said. "You take care."

I hung up, and noticed the patrol car parked ahead of us, the uniform writing a ticket for some poor surfer. I made a U-turn on the Kam and headed back toward the office.

"You going to tell me what happened with this girl?" Ray asked. "Or am I going to have to pry it out of you?"

"Oh. Mindy. So I go over to her apartment that night, and we're talking, and then I hear this key in the door, and within seconds she's all over me. I look up, and this bodybuilder dude is walking in. She says his name is Bobby, and invites him to take his clothes off and join us on the sofa."

"You had no idea that's what was on her mind?"

"None at all. Freaked me out for a minute. I worried the guy was going to punch my lights out for fooling with his girl."

"I presume he didn't."

"Nope. He followed Mindy's instructions, and the rest is history."

Ray laughed. "They say everybody on this island is connected to everybody else," he said, leaning back in his seat. "You're just more connected than most."

9 – Adrift

We stopped at a Zippy's drive-through on our way back to the office. I ordered the Portuguese Bean Soup meal—a rich stew of potatoes, cabbage, beans and ham, along with sides of rice and macaroni salad. Ray tried to go healthy with a salad, but ended up with Korean fried chicken pieces in with his lettuce, tomato, green onions and cucumber.

We were eating at our desks when Salinas stepped in. "Anything new?" he asked.

I had my mouth full of macaroni salad so Ray spoke up, telling him that we had learned Bakir Al-Sarary had done an internship with a shipping company and expressed a lot of interest in learning about security at the port. Once I finished chewing I added what I had learned from Nick Smart and Mindy Kerner.

"So Al-Sarary sounds like he's worth further investigating," Salinas said, nodding. "Good. You'll pass this on to Tomlinson?"

"We'll put together a report as soon as we finish eating."

He pulled up a chair between the two of us and sat down. I had a bad feeling.

"Because of the press attention, this case is heating up, and we're going to have to push for results." He looked at me. "You been keeping up your Japanese?"

When Ray and I had first transferred to the FBI, we'd had to fill out piles of forms and one of the questions asked was foreign language fluency. I was surprised that Salinas remembered I'd indicated a basic knowledge of Japanese—along with high school

French and Hawaiian pidgin.

"I can't read it, but I can ask my way to the bathroom and throw out a couple of choice curses." I saw Ray frowning at my attempt at humor and added, "I can carry on a basic conversation."

"Good enough for government work, as they say." Salinas leaned back. "I am worried that the Japanese may try to cover up any theft of nuclear materials from the Fukushima Dai-Ichi plant, and I need to show that we are taking direct action to solve this case as soon as possible. You've already liaised with the legat in Tokyo, right?"

"I have," Ray said.

"Good. I want you both to go to Japan."

"Really?" I asked. "Japan? Can't the legat handle what we need there?"

Salinas shook his head. "The legat is the Director's personal representative in Japan. That means he reports directly to Headquarters in DC, and I want someone on the ground who reports to me. And the legat is primarily a liaison, not an investigator."

"Do we have any legal authority in Japan?" Ray asked.

"No. However, we regularly conduct complex investigations and acquire evidence from abroad for criminal prosecutions in the United States."

"What specifically do you want us to do?" I asked.

"Start with the legat," Salinas said. "He can get you oriented on the ground. Get as close as you can to the nuclear plant, see what security is like, how that box could have been misplaced. Then head for the town where the Griffins lived. Talk to their family, their friends. I want to know how this couple got hold of those materials, and what the Japanese government is doing to investigate."

"When do you want us to go?" Ray asked.

"There's a non-stop this evening on Hawaiian Air," Salinas said. "I've taken it a couple of times myself. My admin can get you sorted with tickets and hotels." He stood up. "Keep in touch. Either an email or a phone call in advance of the morning meeting."

He walked out. "Julie is going to kill me," Ray said. "Vinnie has been getting bad earaches and we've been taking turns with him. She's going to go ballistic without anybody to help her."

Yeah, and Mike wasn't going to be thrilled that I wouldn't be home for the intimate evening we had planned. But I was excited because I'd never been out of the country before, and I'd be going to my grandfather's homeland. Since our case was going nowhere at home, I hoped Japan would give us a leg up on the investigation.

While Ray called Julie I checked with the admin, who emailed us our itineraries. I looked at the message and realized we had to get a move on.

"We have to be at the airport two hours early for international flights," Ray said.

I looked at my watch. "Crap and double crap." It was almost two. I'd have to hustle to get home, pack, and get to the airport on time. On my way, I called Mike and left him a message. When I got home, I hooked up Roby's leash and took him out for a quick pee, thinking the whole time about what I needed to pack. My cell rang as we were walking back up the driveway.

"You're going to Japan tonight?" Mike asked. "Since when does working for the FBI involve international travel?"

"It's a long story and the trip was not my idea." I opened the front door and unhooked the dog, who scampered across the tile floor to his water bowl to refill his bladder.

"How are you getting to the airport?"

"I need to be there around four-thirty," I said. "Any chance you can drop me?"

"If I move my ass, I suppose."

"And a very cute ass it is," I said. "Thanks."

I hung up. I was excited about the trip, but scared, too. My usual pattern is to rush into things without thinking much, but this was a bigger than normal leap for me. I had never tried to investigate a case when I didn't have jurisdiction.

My thoughts were scattered as I dug around in the closet for my rolling duffle bag. As I began layering shirts and slacks, I realized I had no idea what the weather was like in Japan. A weather site on my phone indicated it was going to be fair and cold in Tokyo, with temperatures in the forties and fifties, which was pretty damn cold for a Hawaiian boy. Then as we moved north to Hakodate it would be even colder, and there would be snow. Living in Hawai'i, we don't have much use for cold-weather clothing. Sure, it can be frigid if you go up to the top of Haleakala on Maui at sunrise—but for the most part we lived in shorts and rubber slippers.

Fortunately for me, Mike had traveled to the mainland several times in the past few years, often in winter, and I was able to raid his side of the closet for scarves, gloves, and a down jacket. By four o'clock I was packed, and pacing nervously around the living room waiting for Mike to show up.

I hadn't told my mother I was going to Japan, so I dug out my cell phone and called her. "*Bonsowa-ru, hahaoya,*" I said when she answered. At Punahou, we had rehearsed the greetings, like good evening, as well as words like mother and father.

"Why are you speaking Japanese?" she asked. "And why is your accent so terrible?" She repeated the words I had said, and they sounded different—much more like the way my teachers had pronounced them. My mother was born and raised in Hawai'i but she spoke fluent Japanese, and there was always an underlying musicality to her language.

I repeated them until I had the sounds more correct. "Ray and I are going to Tokyo on a case," I said. "Tonight."

"Tonight!" she said, and I could hear the alarm in her voice. "Why?"

"You heard about that ship that crashed into the Leeward Coast, didn't you?"

"Oh, that was so terrible! But Japan? Why?"

"Just part of the investigation."

"When are you coming back?"

"I don't know yet, Mom," I said. "I haven't even gotten to the airport yet."

I guess I figured calling my mother would make me feel better about the trip, but it was having the reverse effect.

"What do you mean, you don't know? Don't you have a return ticket?"

"Listen, Mom, Mike is here to drive me. Gotta go. I'll email you from Japan. Love you."

Mike pulled up in the driveway a few minutes later and blew his horn. I petted Roby goodbye and told him to be a good dog for his daddy, and dragged my duffle outside. "You call Dakota?" Mike asked, as he hefted it into his truck. "He'll want to know. And Sandra and Cathy, too."

I hadn't even considered the other important people in my life who'd want to know I was going overseas. "I'll send some texts," I said.

"You can text Cathy. But call Dakota."

I got in beside Mike and dialed Dakota's cell. "Listen, I've got a work emergency," I said when he picked up. "Mike's taking me to the airport now for a flight to Japan."

"You're going to Japan? Awesome. Can you bring me back some cool gay manga?"

"I'm on a case, not a shopping spree, but I'll try."

"Great. I've got a huge web page project to finish. Have fun."

When I hung up, I asked Mike, "Happy now?"

"Let's see. My partner has bailed on the sex we planned for the weekend, and he's heading a thousand miles away to look for nuclear terrorists. No, I'd say I'm not happy."

"If there are terrorists in this case, they're in the U.S., not Japan," I said. "I'm just going there to gather information. No danger involved." That did not mollify Mike, and I had to admit I'd be pissed if he was flying off under similar circumstances.

Mike pulled up in the drop-off zone and I leaned over and kissed his cheek. "I'll be back soon," I said. "Love you."

"Hey, that's not a kiss." He drew me back to him. We locked lips, and I took a moment to breathe in his scent and enjoy the contact. Then he said, "Now, that's a kiss."

"You won't get any argument from me. I expect more where that came from when I get back."

He took my hand. "I'm worried about you, K-Man. You take care of yourself."

"I will." I squeezed his hand, then hopped out and retrieved my backpack and my duffle. I stood there on the curb for a moment, watching him ease back into traffic, before I went inside.

Ray had already checked his bag and was waited for me at the self-check station. Once I handed over my rolling duffle, we walked to the security line, which snaked long beyond the stanchions.

As we moved forward slowly, my cell rang with the KVOL theme—the ring tone I had chosen for my oldest brother. "Coconut telegraph," I said to Ray before I answered. "I told my mother I was going to Japan and she must have called my brother." I took a breath before I pressed the "accept" button and said, "Howzit, brah."

"You're going to Japan?" Lui asked.

"That is a true statement."

"Why? Do you have a lead on that nuclear material?"

"You know I can't tell you, Lui," I said, as the line shuffled forward.

"I don't expect you to reveal your whole case," Lui said. "Just give me a teaser I can use on the news."

"I have two words for you. Randy. Vernon."

"I don't need to call the press liaison," he said. "I can call my little brother. The one who owes me about a million favors."

"Oops, gotta go," I said. "I'm up to the TSA checkpoint. See you when I get back."

I ended the call, and for good measure I turned my phone off and stowed it in my backpack. Just to make a liar of me, the line stalled, and we stood there for a couple of minutes before we went forward even a foot.

As we got close, Ray pulled out his passport and boarding pass and I did the same. He noticed how beat up his looked compared to mine. "New passport?" he asked.

"Yeah. My first. I'm glad Salinas suggested I get it when I started at the Bureau."

"You didn't have one already?"

"Never needed one before," I said.

"Seriously? You've never been OCONUS?"

I elbowed him. "Don't start with those acronyms. In the first place, in case you've forgotten your geography, Hawai'i is outside the continental United States. And no, I've never been to a foreign country. But I presume you have?"

"I did a junior semester in Italy," he said. "University of Bologna. After that I got hooked on Europe. Julie and I have been all over the place." He slung an arm around my shoulder. "Don't worry, I'll look after you."

I squirmed away. "I already have two big brothers. Don't need a third."

When we reached the TSA agent checking ID, I handed her my boarding pass and passport. She pried it open and I heard the spine crack. Suddenly it hit me: I was leaving the U.S. for a foreign country, with only a vague sense of what I was supposed to be doing. I followed Ray down the corridor toward our departure gate in a daze. How was I going to manage? I had told Salinas that I could carry on a conversation in Japanese, and I had been able to fumble my way along with witnesses and suspects when no translator was available. But when my mom's family gathered and she began speaking rapid Japanese with her sisters, I had been lost.

In Honolulu, I relied on my intimate knowledge of the city, the island and its people. I knew the right shortcuts to take through Chinatown and Waikiki. I almost always knew someone who knew someone who could provide me with information.

In Japan, I wouldn't have any of those advantages. It would be a real test of my skill as an investigator to see if I could discover anything at all.

We made it to the departure gate just as they were beginning to board. As we waited in line, Ray yawned. "Between Vinnie's earaches and all our running around this week, I'm beat. As soon as I get to my seat I'm opening up my pillow, popping a pill, and sleeping for the next eight and a half hours."

"What do you mean, opening up?"

He pulled a bundle of plastic from his backpack. "This unfolds and blows up to be a whole-seat cushion," he said. "Better for sleeping."

"You've got this whole thing figured out," I said admiringly.

We trudged onward. The plane was huge and I was sitting way in the back, in a middle seat. A wizened haole woman with flyaway white hair was by the window, a middle-aged man in a business suit at the aisle.

The man stood to let me in, and the woman said, "Why are you getting up, Michael?"

"This guy has the middle seat, Mother," he said to her, speaking the way my mom had spoken to my dad, loud and clear.

"If you'd rather sit next to each other," I began, but the man cut me off.

"She likes the window, I like the aisle."

I squeezed in between them. For the rest of the flight, they bickered across me. He had to hand her a tissue, a newspaper, ask her what she wanted to drink. Every time I found a comfortable position, he was reaching across me with something. When the crew turned down the cabin lights I tried to doze off, but the old lady's rippling snores woke me every time.

By the time the plane landed I knew why I had never traveled abroad before. It was just too far. I stood up and bumped my head on the bulkhead, then tried to shake out the cramps in my arms and legs. The flight attendant told us that the local time was ten p.m. and I was disoriented. Shouldn't it be the next morning?

Ray was waiting for me at the gate. "Hold this for me?" he asked, thrusting his backpack at me. I put mine down on the carpet and took his, as he folded up his inflatable pillow and stuffed it inside. "*Domo arigato, Mr. Roboto*," he sang, as he took the backpack from me. I recognized the line from the Styx song.

"You're awfully cheerful," I grumbled.

"Slept like a log. Now we have to get our bags and go through Customs. We got lucky with our flight—if we'd flown in to Narita we'd have an hour-long train ride into Tokyo. As it is, we can just get a cab."

"You're not going to be this cheerful the whole time we're here, are you? Because I might have to kill you."

The airport was surprisingly busy for so late at night. Throngs of Asian men in business suits and women with multi-colored hair streamed past us. Because my father and my brothers were as tall as I was, and Mike was even taller, I didn't have much sense back home of being, at six-one, all that tall. But among those Japanese I stood out like a longboard planted in the sand.

Ray and I trudged along past tall glass windows and endless rows of small lights, past lit signs in kanji characters, a shop with a pagoda-like roof. It was strange and yet familiar at the same time. Would the whole country be like this? Or would we have trouble navigating? Suppose we got lost, and Ray looked to me to translate. Would I be able to manage?

"We have to stop at that counter," Ray said, pointing at a kiosk decorated with posters of pagodas and mountains. "We can get two weeks of free Wi-Fi all over the country if we show our passports."

I marveled at how much he had learned in such a short time. After we got our cards, with individual access codes, I followed Ray toward the taxi rank. Maybe it was the jet lag or the lack of sleep, or just the fact that I had never been anywhere like Japan, but I felt adrift. How was I going to investigate a crime in a country where every step forward was confusing?

10 – Zone Change

Our cab driver didn't speak English, but he understood Hotel Okura. "Reminds me of Times Square in New York," Ray said, as the driver zipped through the still-busy streets. "All the neon, the traffic, the crowds of people out late."

I wished I could share his enthusiasm. But I was worried about our ability to operate in Japan, and I already missed Mike. Ray handled the check-in with the English-speaking desk clerk, asking for my passport, showing me where to sign. And then we were blessedly in our double room, and I dropped my bags on the floor and collapsed on the bed.

"I could sleep for hours," I said.

He pulled a pill bottle from his bag. "Take two of these," he said. "Melatonin. We crossed four time zones, heading west. That means we'll need about two days to get our body clocks back in synch. Melatonin will help."

"If you say so."

Ray used the bathroom, and then I did, and I stripped down and climbed between the sheets. He was already asleep but I lay there getting accustomed to everything that had happened in the last three days, from my first look at that sailboat to landing at Haneda Airport. If this assignment continued at the same pace, could I manage to keep up? And then I was out.

I woke to bright light streaming in through the window. Ray stood beside it, staring out at the sunrise. "What time is it?" I grumbled.

"Seven-thirty. Honolulu is nineteen hours behind us, so it's about one thirty in the afternoon there. Thursday. It's already Friday morning here. We lost a day crossing the International Date Line." He was wearing shorts, a T-shirt and running shoes, and he leaned down to touch his toes.

It was all baffling to me. I had enough trouble navigating the time differences between Honolulu and the mainland, calculating whether the rest of the country was on daylight savings time, and what the zone was where I was calling.

"The Embassy doesn't open 'til eight-thirty so I'm going down to the gym," Ray said. "You want to come?"

I sat up. "There's a gym?"

"Sure. Come down and meet me if you want."

I should have gotten up to work out. But instead I turned over and went back to sleep, only waking when Ray touched me on the shoulder. He had a towel around his waist and was using another to dry his hair. "Better get up," he said. "We can grab a quick breakfast downstairs and then get to the Embassy around nine. Don't want them to take us for a couple of slackers."

I sat up and stretched. "I've got Skype on my phone," Ray said. "And we've got Wi-Fi here in the hotel. I already spoke to Julie. You want to call Mike?"

"I thought our phones wouldn't work here. Aren't they incompatible or something?"

"Skype uses the Internet, not the local phone network. So as long as we have Wi-Fi we can make calls. Give me Mike's cell number and I'll dial it for you."

"I have to check my phone. I don't have it memorized."

Ray groaned. "Is this what you're like when you don't have Harry Ho around to navigate technology for you?"

"Give me a break," I grumbled. "I lost a day somewhere and I don't know where it went." I dug my phone out, waited for it to turn on, and then read Mike's phone number off to Ray. He dialed, then handed the phone to me.

"Riccardi, HFD."

"Mike? It's me. You sound like you're a million miles away."

"Why didn't you call me when you landed? I was worried about you."

"Slow down, cowboy. I'm dislocated here. I didn't even realize we could use the phone until Ray showed me. And you could have checked the airline website."

"I did. But it would have been nice to hear from you."

"Sorry. How's everything back home?"

"Roby had diarrhea this morning. I found a hole in my favorite khakis. I'm investigating two different fires at opposite ends of the island. And I miss you."

Ray stood beside me. "Kiss kiss, bye bye," he said. "We've got to get moving."

"I miss you too," I said to Mike. "Now that I know how this works, I'll call you later, when Ray isn't hovering around me. Love you."

He said he loved me too, and then I ended the call and handed the phone back to Ray. I felt better after a shower, though I was still jet-lagged. Downstairs we had a choice of Japanese or European breakfast; Ray got scrambled eggs, bacon and toast, but I went for my childhood comfort foods—steamed rice, miso soup, and a *tamagoyaki*, a rolled omelet with daikon radish on the side.

"You're going native fast," Ray said, surveying my plate.

"Remember, my mom's father was Japanese," I said. "This is the kind of food she used to cook for us when we were kids."

"How did Salinas know you spoke Japanese?" he asked, between bites. "You put that on your application?"

"Salinas knows everything about us," I said. "Down to those tighty-whities you wear. I gave up on those when I reached puberty."

"I can't wear boxers," he protested. "My boys bounce around too much."

I laughed. "Your boys?"

"Seriously. How much Japanese do you know?"

"I can make basic conversation," I said. "I've forgotten a lot of words I'm sure will come back. I took four years of the language at Punahou but I don't get much chance to use it except eavesdropping on Harry's wife Arleen talking to her mother."

I finished the last scoop of rice. "But I can't read kanji. So we're going to have to depend on English to get around."

When we left the hotel, the cold hit me like a slap in the face, and I huddled into Mike's down coat, which was a couple of inches too long for me. We both had our laptop computers with us; mine was in my backpack, slung over one shoulder. Ray and I walked over to the Embassy, a sleek, multi-story office building, and by the time we got there I was sweating and I was glad to shag off the bulky coat.

Jutta Dore, the legat Ray had spoken with, met us in the lobby and signed for us. He was a dark-haired guy with slightly Asian features, and I figured he was a mix like me. He had to be about forty, and there were touches of gray in his manicured sideburns.

"How was your trip?" he asked, as the elevator rose.

"Long flight," I said. "Feeling kind of jet-lagged."

"I know the drill," he said. "Flying back and forth to DC is hell on air."

The doors opened and he led us down the hall to his office. "From the analysis of the material on the boat, I figured it had to be something that would have been very toxic to whoever handled it," he said, as we walked into a small office decorated with plaques and commendations.

"That isn't quite correct," Ray said. "What we've discovered is that the plutonium would have been safe as long as it was completely sealed. The Griffins died because the box was damaged and the plutonium contaminated the air in the boat."

Dore looked deflated. "Well, even if it was a flawed assumption, I believe that it turned up some useful information. I did a search for any managers who died of radiation-related illness in the time since the incident."

We sat down across from his desk. "The government tries to keep this information hush-hush, but I found at least a half-dozen deaths, and I asked a contact in the Japanese government to take a look at the financial records for all of them. He hit pay dirt on Akiro Suzuki, a senior maintenance specialist for unit three. A week after the meltdown, Suzuki received a transfer of five million yen from an account in the Cayman Islands."

"How much is that in dollars?" I asked.

"About fifty grand," Dore said. "Not a lot by ordinary standards, but a big boost for a worker like Suzuki."

"Unit Three?" I asked, remembering the information I had found with Mike. "Isn't that the one that used mixed-oxide fuel?"

"Exactly," Dore said. "So he would have had access to the plutonium oxide you found on the boat."

"Have you been able to trace that account in the Caymans?" I asked.

"I put through an official request. Because of the national security risk, I can get some traction, but it's going to take time. In the meantime, the three of us could go up to Fukushima and talk to Suzuki's widow, see what she has to say." He looked at his watch. "It's about a ninety-minute train trip from Tokyo."

"Sounds good to me," I said. "But why haven't you been to see her already?"

"Just got the information yesterday, and I figured you'd want to be involved in any interviews. So I waited."

Dore picked up his phone and put on a pair of reading glasses, then reached for a folder and opened it. He dialed a number and I did my best to eavesdrop, but he spoke quickly and with an odd accent, and I could only catch a couple of words. I figured out that he was speaking to a woman, and assumed it was the widow of the dead plant manager.

"*Arrigato gozeimasu,*" he said to the woman, then hung up. He turned to his computer and typed, then looked back at us. "Mrs.

Suzuki can see us this afternoon at four. There's a two-fifteen train on the Tohoku Shinkansen line to Fukushima that should get us there just in time. The Shinkansen lines are on the east side of the station. Why don't we meet in front of the Daimaru department store at two?"

I looked at Ray, and he nodded. "Sounds good to us. Is there anyone else in Tokyo you think we should talk to? About security at the plant? Any police here we should make contact with?"

"I'd rather you didn't have direct contact with the police at this time," he said. "I've already put out some feelers about plant security and police response, and I'll let you know what I discover."

It wasn't the answer we wanted, but I remembered that Salinas had said that Dore reported directly to the FBI director, and didn't want to antagonize him so quickly. We stood up, shook hands with Dore, and then he led us back to the elevator.

"What do you want to do now?" Ray asked me as we rode down. "Any ideas on places we need to go, people we need to talk to?"

I felt that same sense of loss and dislocation. I could barely remember how to get back to the hotel. How could I look around Tokyo for information?"

"Dore is the only contact we have right now," I said. "And he doesn't want us snooping around on his turf, so I think we have to trust him for the moment. Salinas wanted us to look into how the materials could have been stolen from the reactor, and we're going to talk to this Suzuki woman about that."

"And he wanted us to go up to Hakodate and talk to members of Chikako's family," Ray said.

"Crap," I said. "Salinas told us to check in with him before the morning meeting each day. But it's already long past that." We walked outside, and the cold air hit me again. "I need some kind of hot beverage to warm up. Why don't we find a coffee shop with Wi-Fi and call in to the office, see if anything new has come up?"

From where we stood I could see three different coffee shops within a block. We chose one called Doutor and stood in a long line, giving us ample time to evaluate the menu and all the signage. "Look at that," I said, pointing to one poster. Though I couldn't read the kanji, I recognized the coffee plantations on the Kona coast. "We flew all the way across the Pacific to get coffee grown in Hawai'i."

I ordered a cappuccino for Ray and a café mocha for myself, pleased that the clerk understood my butchered Japanese. When we got our drinks we sat down at a table and used our phones and the cards we'd gotten at the airport to access the free Wi-Fi. "An email from Emily Sukihara," I said as I clicked it open. "A work address for Chikako's sister, and home address for the parents. No phone numbers. No other names." I looked up at him. "This is the best the Bureau can do?"

"Got the same message," he said. "So nobody back there could find any leads for us to follow here in Tokyo."

"That's frustrating," I said. "We flew all this way when Dore could have spoken to Mrs. Suzuki himself and reported back to us."

"Hold your horses, tiger," Ray said. "Assuming we don't learn anything this afternoon that keeps us in Tokyo, we'll head to Hakodate tomorrow."

It was a reasonable plan and I tried to relax, but I kept thinking about those two dead babies and their parents, and I itched to learn why they had died. Ray and I collaborated on an email to Salinas for the next morning meeting in Kapolei, indicating that we had made contact with Jutta Dore and had the interview with Mrs. Suzuki that afternoon.

Once that was out of the way, I sipped my coffee and read an email from Mike, then typed one back to him. Before I sent it, I copied a big chunk and then pasted that into a message to my mother and my brothers.

"So what next?" Ray asked, when we both had packed up our laptops.

I shrugged. "Go back to the hotel and hang out?"

"Are you crazy? We're in Tokyo and we've got five hours to see the city. Let's go do something Japanese." He began to sing again, this time the song by the one-hit wonders The Vapors. "I'm turning Japanese, I think I'm turning Japanese, I really think so."

"You know that song is all about masturbation, don't you?" I said, as we stepped back out into the cold. "The way your eyes squint like a Japanese man's as you get close to orgasm." I squinted my eyes shut and opened my mouth.

"Good to see you got your sense of humor back." He pulled a sheaf of paper from his back pocket. "I printed out some pages about sight-seeing in Tokyo. I think we could catch a *futsudensha* train—that's the local, the *kaisokudensha* is the express—from here to the Meiji Shrine, and then another to the Imperial Palace, which would leave us close to Tokyo Station around the time we need to meet Dore."

His pronunciation sounded a lot better than mine. "How do you know all this?"

"They're called maps," he said, holding up a pocket-sized one. "Ever use one?"

I didn't, because I had lived my whole life on O'ahu and knew how to get around. And I'd gotten spoiled by GPS directions—just plug an address into my phone, and it would tell me how to get there.

"You can be the tour guide, then," I said.

He led the way to the station, and together we figured out which line to take and how much money the tickets would be. I'd always heard that the Tokyo subways jammed people in like sardines, but riding that day with Ray I learned I'd underestimated the situation. They had staff on the platform pushing people inside long after I'd have thought the train was full.

I could see why the Japanese had developed a culture of exaggerated politeness—you needed it if you were going to be jammed up against someone in a very intimate position. My nose was a few inches from another straphanger's armpit and my groin pushed uncomfortably against another man's butt for about ten minutes. I thought about math problems to keep from embarrassing myself.

We stumbled out of the car at the Meiji Shrine station, pulled along on by a tide of humanity. I didn't take a deep breath until we were outside again. Cigarette smoke and automobile exhaust had never smelled so good before.

"We need to find the offering box," Ray said, as we approached the towering torii gate. Ahead of us I could see the gently sloping roofs and the bright red parasols of other visitors. "It's near the big taiko drum. You know what one of those looks like?"

"Sure. Why are we making an offering?"

"Good luck. If you want, you can write down a prayer and stick it on the wall." As we got closer, he pointed toward a wall with rows of paper offerings pinned to it. "But I figure since neither of us can write kanji we're better off just speaking."

I felt overwhelmed by the culture around me. This was the land of my forefathers, even if only on one side. I had always felt at home in Hawai'i, confident in knowing it was where I belonged. But what if things had played out differently for Ojisan, and he had remained in Japan? Then he would never have married my Hawaiian grandmother, and my mother and I would never have been born.

Or, if you subscribed to a different set of beliefs, then my mother might have been born in Japan, with only half her existing genetic makeup. She's fiercely ambitious, so I doubted she'd have been happy as a farm wife. She might have gone on to marry a salaryman, someone as intelligent as she was, and perhaps even had three sons, in that life. I had always believed that so much of who I was came from my father, and my Hawaiian heritage. I couldn't see myself growing up in Japan, becoming obedient to my family and my culture. And yet, I could not help being moved by this land and its people.

Ray and I found the drum and the offering box. "Bow your head twice, clap twice, and bow once more," Ray said. "And you think about what you want."

I knew what Ray would pray for, and my own prayers were much the same. I prayed for safety for my family and friends, and a long and happy life for Addie and Owen. I prayed for myself as well; I hoped that spending time in Ojisan's homeland would help me get to

Neil S. Plakcy

know that Japanese part of myself, whatever it was.

I had Ray take a picture of me in front of the temple for my mother. When I looked at it, I saw that I was surrounded by a sea of faces that looked much like mine. Ray must have noticed the same thing, because he said, "You're starting to look more Japanese the more time we spend here."

A chilly wind swept over us as we left the temple grounds, and I adjusted Mike's scarf around my neck, and a comforting whiff of his aftershave rose around my face.

We continued to joke as we slid our fare cards and then navigated our way to the right train—or what we hoped was the right one. I couldn't help feeling that we were running our investigation like a vacation—sightseeing when we should have been talking to suspects or looking for clues. But I couldn't wrap my head around what we were missing.

"I wonder why Dore wants to come with us to see Mrs. Suzuki?" I asked as we waited. "Just to translate?"

"Do you think we need him? Could you manage enough Japanese to interview her yourself?"

"I downloaded a Japanese translation app to my phone for whenever there's a word I don't know. And the more I hear people speaking, the more words come back to me. If she spoke slowly and clearly, I could get the point."

"It's not just about the language," Ray said. "Back in Hawai'i we can tell if someone's lying, or being evasive, by body language. Here it's all different."

I had to agree with Ray. We had both taken courses in interpreting body language through HPD—things like shifting eyes, arms crossed and so on. "Japanese people think it's rude to look you in the eyes," I said. "And so much of the nuance of a conversation is conveyed through silence, pauses, facial expressions. Not to mention the whole bowing thing—I think the person of the lower status is supposed to bow lower, but how do we figure that out?"

"Julie says that women bow with their hands on the front of their

–80–

legs, while men bow with their hands at their sides."

Julie had completed her MA in Pacific Islands Studies at UH and then a PhD in American Studies, continuing the research she had begun on the effects of ethnic background on consumer purchasing decisions. Things had been iffy for her and Ray after she graduated; there weren't many teaching jobs in her field, and I had worried they'd pick up and leave Hawai'i so she could take a job somewhere.

But then she had snared a job with a consulting firm that advised corporations in the region, and she was able to use her research skills for demographic studies and reports. "Since Julie knows so much about Japan, maybe I should have brought her with me instead of you."

"And leave me home with Vinnie and his earaches? Not on your life."

The train arrived and we jammed ourselves in. We couldn't talk again until we had gotten off at Tokyo Station, and the first thing I heard as we rode a long escalator to the surface was my stomach grumbling. It was getting close to noon, so I led Ray to a street vendor near the Imperial Palace, attracted by the aroma of chicken on a charcoal grill.

For the first time since our arrival, I felt like I knew what I was doing. I ordered yakitori for both of us, bite-sized pieces of chicken skewered on bamboo. I stuck to the *toriniku*, all white meat, avoiding the cartilage, liver and gizzards. From another stand we bought *gyoza*, dumplings stuffed with meat and vegetables, with a thicker skin than pot stickers. We topped it off with Ramune brand soda—I got the melon flavor, and Ray the strawberry.

Our bellies full, we strolled alongside a moat surrounding the original Edo Castle. I wanted to think of myself as the modern equivalent of a samurai, but in ancient Japanese society I would have been confined to the class of my ancestors. Not for the first time I was grateful that Ojisan had braved the Pacific and come to Hawai'i in search of a better life for himself and his family.

The Japanese were a people deeply rooted in their personal histories, so I believed that my family had been farmers for centuries before my grandfather's birth. Though there was always a chance that a royal prince who had once lived in this palace had been exiled in the distant past, moved to Shikoku, and begun a line of descent that ended with me.

In this life, though, I was a cop investigating a crime. "This sightseeing is fun," I said to Ray. "But we need to do something related to our case."

"I agree," he said. "But realistically, we don't have any leads to follow. Maybe this Mrs. Suzuki can point us toward other managers or rank and file."

We strolled around the temple, marveling at the forbidding stone walls and the peaked roofs, and Ray took a lot more pictures for Julie. I was fascinated to see a part of my heritage that I'd never paid much attention to. As a kid, I had gone to Hawaiian language and culture school in the afternoons, and of course I'd been steeped in haole culture by virtue of being an American citizen.

But many Hawaiians had an ambivalent or even negative attitude toward Japan, after the attack on Pearl Harbor, the reputation that the "made in Japan" mark had for crappy workmanship when I was a kid, then the huge investment in Hawaiian real estate by wealthy Japanese. So my family had kept our Japanese heritage under wraps for the most part, though we had observed the occasional holiday like Boys' Day in May, when we flew three banners in the shape of carp—the largest for Lui, the smallest for me.

Looking at the stone walls and ramparts, the remnants of Edo Castle, I was intrigued to know more. Perhaps the real purpose of this trip would be to investigate my own connection to Japanese culture, rather than to find out how that radioactive material had ended up on the Usagi Maru.

I doubted Francisco Salinas or the FBI leadership would go along with that, though.

11 – Tea with the Widow

We made our way to the department store a few minutes early, and stood on the sidewalk watching the crowds. I was struck by how much uniformity there was. Almost everyone we saw was ethnic Japanese. Both men and women wore business suits, though there was more variation on the female side—occasionally a woman's suit might be white, instead of the standard black or navy. It was such a contrast to Hawai'i, where haoles, Asians and native Hawaiians mixed freely with a sprinkling of black and brown faces.

Dore arrived, and led us from the store through the intricate maze of the train station. He spoke to the clerk, then handed us our tickets. "You speak Japanese very well," I asked Dore as we walked toward the track. "Where'd you learn?"

"My mom's Japanese," he said. "She went to Cornell on a student visa and met my dad there. He came from a long line of Finns who settled that area. They got married and I grew up there. I learned Finnish from my grandfather and Japanese from my mother."

"An odd combination," I said.

"Tell me about it. When I graduated from college I had a choice between the FBI and the CIA. I chose the Bureau. I was the legat in Helsinki for a couple of years, and then transferred here last year."

The train that pulled in was sleek and silver, with a long snout that reminded me of Roby's. Though we'd only been gone a few days, I felt homesick, missing my partner, my kids, my dog.

Once on board, Dore pulled out a netbook and began to read, and Ray and I looked out the windows for a while as the urban sprawl of

Tokyo skimmed by. Every building was jammed against its neighbor, and the streets were narrow and winding. New skyscrapers next to older low buildings, neon signs so close they blended together.

The closeness was the consequence of living on an island, something I knew all too well. But there were a lot more people shoehorned into Honshu, the seventh-largest island in the world, than O'ahu, and I marveled at how every street was jammed with cars and pedestrians.

It took a long time to leave the city behind and even out in the countryside I could see the effects of civilization everywhere, from the ancient terraced fields to modern satellite dishes. I turned to Dore. "What kind of questions do we have for this woman?"

"I want to know how that chunk of money ended up in her husband's bank account," Dore said. "I'd like to know if he was discontented at work, if he knew how sick he was, and if he had connections to anyone who dealt in contraband materials. But I can't come right out and ask those questions, or she'll shut right down. So I suggest you both keep quiet unless something jumps out at you."

I wanted to respond with a snarky comment, but I resisted. He went back to his netbook, and I asked Ray if he had a guidebook I could borrow.

He handed me a couple of the printed pages, reserving a few for himself, and we both read until we approached Fukushima City. The train tracks were lined with cherry, peach, pears and apple trees. "They call Fukushima the Kingdom of Fruits," Dore said, putting away his netbook. "That mountain up ahead is Mt. Shinobu-yama, which is the city's symbol. Lots of traditional temples up there, and apparently great views of the city. I haven't been but I have a friend who used to vacation here."

When the train pulled into the station, Dore led us to a taxi rank and slipped into the front seat of a yellow cab with funny-looking right and left mirrors attached to the hood. He gave the cabbie the address and we took off through streets that were only marginally less crowded than Tokyo's. We passed a line of small children wearing matching blue and white uniforms and holding hands. Some things were the same all over the world.

We pulled up at a grim-looking concrete apartment building. The lobby was festooned with painted cartoon animals, though, and the elevator and corridors were scrupulously clean. We rode up to the tenth floor and Dore led us to apartment 1010, where Etsu Suzuki invited us into her home.

She was tall for a Japanese woman, and she wore a black *yukata*, a type of simple, unlined kimono. Hers was decorated with silver cranes that picked up the graying threads in her hair. She wore *geta* sandals, with square blocks to raise the hem of the yukata off the floor, and white *tabi* socks.

She and Dore bowed to each other, and he introduced us. Then she led us into her living room, where she had laid out a tea service on a low coffee table between two sofas. I sat beside Dore on one, with Ray across from us and next to Mrs. Suzuki.

Behind her was a photo of her and the man I assumed was her late husband, Akiro. Though they were in casual clothing and it looked like they were on vacation with a beach behind them, Akiro did not look happy. His face was thin and lined and he stood a step away from his wife.

I was able to follow the conversation at first—Mrs. Suzuki hoped we had enjoyed a pleasant train ride, commented on the weather and so on. When we all had our tea, Dore began speaking to her in more rapid, complicated Japanese, and I could only catch occasional words.

Every so often he would stop and translate for us. "A few months before the tsunami, Mr. Suzuki was diagnosed with pancreatic cancer. His wife believes that it was caused by his work at the plant."

I felt sad. A college friend's father had died of pancreatic cancer, which can be quick and quite often incurable.

"Mrs. Suzuki does not know where the large deposit to her husband's bank account came from," Dore continued. "He paid all the bills until the last days of his illness, when he began to show her how to write checks and manage finances."

I knew that there must have been a great deal of chaos at the plant, after the earthquake, and then the succeeding tsunami which flooded the area around the backup generators. Many workers had struggled to restore power to the cooling systems and control rooms. Was Akiro Suzuki one of those? Had that access given him the opportunity to steal the nuclear materials. But how, and why?

"Can you ask her what her husband did after the tsunami hit the reactors?" I asked.

He nodded, and launched into a long question. She pulled a tissue from her yukata halfway through the conversation and began dabbing at her eyes. I felt bad that we were putting this poor widow through an explanation of her husband's death, but there was no way around it.

Dore turned back to us. "Her husband was a good and loyal employee," he said. "He put himself at great risk, going back into the plant after the quarantine to make sure that more damage did not occur."

I said, in what I hoped was proper Japanese, that we were very sorry for her loss. Then I asked what kind of work her husband did at the plant.

She spoke in a rush, so fast that I could only get the general gist. He had been a manager at the Unit 3 Reactor, responsible for supervising the workers who maintained the cooling equipment—the one that had used plutonium.

Akiro Suzuki had the opportunity to the steal the plutonium, the means to do so, and the motive—to provide for his widow.

I asked Dore, "Did her husband ever bring anything home from the plant that had hazard markings?"

He asked her, and she looked down at the contents of her teacup, as if the leaves there would tell her what to say.

"Tell Mrs. Suzuki that we know her husband was a good man, and that he was only trying to provide for her after his death," I said.

When he had finished, she looked up at him and began to speak. I caught enough to know that he had brought a sealed box home one evening a few days after the meltdown, and had stored it in the back of a closet for a long time. Only when he became very sick and stopped working did he take the box away. She had been worried and nervous, so she searched his pants afterwards, and discovered a ticket to the town of Nihonmatsu. She asked him why he went there, but he would not say. A few weeks later he was dead.

Dore looked sad, and gave her time to collect herself. He asked her a few more questions, but it was clear that she had no idea why he had gone to Nihonmatsu, or who he had met there.

We stood and thanked her for her time. I repeated my condolences, and Ray nodded in agreement. When we were in the elevator Dore said, "The Nihonmatsu connection is a very bad sign."

"Why? Who or what was in Nihonmatsu?" I asked.

"After the earthquake, the Japanese government was slow to move resources into Fukushima to help people. The Yamaguchi-gumi, one of the three largest criminal syndicates, sent hundreds of trucks filled with supplies to the area. Nihonmatsu was one of their staging areas. From what I understand they maintained a significant presence there long afterwards."

"She didn't want to tell you that, because she knew that it meant her husband was going to meet with yakuza," I said.

"Hold on," Ray said. "I'm a couple of steps behind you here. The yakuza were providing aid instead of the government?"

Dore nodded. "Smart move on their part, because it established a lot of goodwill."

"You think Suzuki went to Nihonmatsu to sell the material he stole from the plant to the yakuza?" Ray asked.

"The yakuza have had a long history of involvement with the nuclear industry," Dore said. "There are no mandatory background checks for industry workers. So it's very possible that Suzuki worked with yakuza members. Once he had the plutonium in hand, he could have contacted someone he knew from the plant to arrange a sale to some middleman, who then made the deal with the eventual buyer, who was expecting the shipment to arrive on the Usagi Maru."

My brain was going a mile a minute making connections. The elevator landed on the first floor of Mrs. Suzuki's apartment building and we stepped out. I held the door for a young mother with two kids in a stroller. By the time I caught up to Ray and Dore they were on the street and Dore was on the phone.

According to the Usagi Maru's log, the Griffins had spent a few days in Shiogama just before they left for Hawai'i. How close was that to Nihonmatsu? I'd have to look it up on a map as soon as I had internet access.

Dore ended his call and said, "A cab is on its way." He slipped his phone into his pocket. "The sad fact is that because of the yakuza infiltration into the nuclear industry, a domestic terrorist here could easily get access to the materials necessary to build and detonate a nuclear dirty bomb, kill thousands of people, and render a lot of the country uninhabitable."

"But surely the government knows that," Ray said.

Dore shrugged. "The Nuclear Regulation Authority is studying atomic energy security issues. They hope to have recommendations in place for background checks within the next couple of years. But the yakuza have secret alliances with various government officials who could stall the process."

How could you operate in a country with so many conflicting interests? Oh, wait. Sounded a lot like the United States. "Can you put a trace on Suzuki's calls and his emails to see if you can find out who he went to Nihonmatsu to meet with?" I asked.

"That will have to go through the Keisatsu-chō," he said, naming Japan's national police agency. He looked at his watch. "It's too late to get anything started with them today. I'll get in touch with my contact there on Monday morning."

As the cab navigated back to the train station, I looked out the window. The streets buzzed with energy, salarymen in their dark suits hurrying along the sidewalks, teenaged girls with neon-colored hair and earbuds, the occasional older woman in a simple yukata like the one Etsu Suzuki had worn.

As we waited in the ticket line at the train station, Ray asked Dore,

"Where do we go from here?"

"We go back to Tokyo," Dore said. "It's Friday afternoon and you're not going to get much information from official sources over the weekend."

"You don't seem to be taking this very seriously," I said.

"On the contrary, I take this quite seriously," Dore said. "This is a high-profile situation. Much larger than you and I and your investigation. Japanese nuclear material headed for unknown operatives on the U.S. mainland? It's a diplomatic time bomb. But the way we work in the Bureau is to push things like this uphill. I'll make a full report of what I heard from Mrs. Suzuki and then wait for instructions. I suggest you do the same."

I didn't like being reprimanded, and I was uncertain whether Jutta Dore was a good guy or just another bureaucrat, but for a change I kept my mouth shut.

He bought the tickets and handed one to each of us, then pulled out his phone again. Ray and I browsed the kiosks. Most of the written material was in kanji, with only the occasional headline in English, and I remembered we were in a foreign country with only our Bureau contacts to help us.

I saw one of those Doutor coffee shops and turned to Ray. "I don't want to sit on my ass waiting for Jutta Dore to tell me what to do," I said. "I have some stuff I want to look up online while we wait for the train. Want to get a coffee with me?"

I mimed coffee to Dore, and he shook his head. Ray went up to the counter to order our drinks and I used the access card I got at the airport to check Google Maps. "It's about two hours by train from Nihonmatsu to Shiogama," I said.

Ray nodded. "So maybe a yakuza from Nihonmatsu delivered the plutonium to Shiogama, and Dale and Chikako took the boat there to retrieve it."

"Dore said that the money came into Suzuki's bank account a few weeks before he died, which corresponds with what his widow said about the timing of his trip to Nihonmatsu. Can you look up exactly when that was?"

While Ray did that, I opened the Usagi Maru's log. Before we left Hawai'i, I had scanned it and uploaded the PDF to my laptop. Between the two of us, we established that the Griffins had picked up the box in Shiogama in November of 2015, a month after Suzuki's death.

We finished our coffee and rejoined Dore as the train pulled in. "What are you two planning to do over the weekend?" he asked, as we settled into seats.

"We're going up to Hakodate," I said. "Our Japanese language specialist came up with a list of Chikako Griffin's family and friends. We'll talk to each of them and see what they know about the Griffins' trip."

"You sure that's a good idea?" Dore asked. "Hakodate's a backwater, and I doubt people will talk to strangers, especially white guys who don't speak the language."

"We can get by," I said, once again irritated by Dore's attitude. "I'm remembering more Japanese every day. Ray can get us anyplace we need to go, and the two of us are experienced investigators. Even back in Hawai'i, you know, people don't like to talk to the cops, and we still find out what we need to know."

Dore's attitude reminded me of many Bureau agents I'd worked with as a cop. Some agents felt that they were the only ones competent to carry out an investigation. Well, Dore hadn't seen the dynamic team of Kanapa'aka and Donne in action.

12 – Of the Bureau

We left Dore back where we had met him, in front of the Daimaru department store. "You mind if we make a detour inside to do some shopping?" Ray asked. "I'd like to get something for Julie."

It was like shopping at the Shirokiya department store back at Ala Moana Center, only without the English subtitles that the store management put up for Americans. Ray picked out a yukata for Julie in a beautiful cherry-blossom print, shades of pink, white and red. I bought a black one with a red and orange flame pattern for Mike, and a video-game patterned one for Dakota. The yukata Ray chose for himself was stately, in navy blue with white bamboo, but I went for goofy, an ukiyo-e print of male kabuki players.

We bought a couple of folding fans in bright patterns, and I got some Hello Kitty outfits for Addie and Owen. Ray sprang for cute Japanese wooden toys for Vinnie and a mask like a demonic motorcyclist. I remembered the twins on the boat—that their parents would never have a chance to buy toys for them again, that all the love Dale and Chikako felt for their babies had evaporated into the tainted air along with their last breaths.

We staggered back to the hotel with our purchases like successful hunter-gatherers. At least we'd managed something, even if we weren't moving the case forward very well.

"The yakuza are serious criminals," Ray said, as we collapsed onto our beds.

"Like smuggling nuclear material isn't serious? We knew this case was going to get nasty."

"Doesn't it freak you out?" he asked.

"Of course it does. But like Dore said, we push things uphill at the Bureau. You and I just focus on the Griffins and we let the higher-ups figure out the really bad stuff."

We spent the next half-hour on our laptops, putting down everything we'd learned, along with a list of questions. Dore would follow up on the Cayman Islands account where the money for Suzuki had come from, and the trace on Suzuki's phone records. The local police had already notified Chikako's family of her death, but Ray and I would go to Hakodate and meet as many people as we could who knew Dale and Chikako Griffin and ask questions about their yakuza connections and what they'd said before they left for the trans-Pacific trip.

When we finished, Ray emailed the report to Salinas. He lent me his phone, and I walked over to the window that looked out on the busy street to call Mike.

It was almost bedtime on Thursday night back in Honolulu, and as Mike told me about the fire he'd been investigating, I could hear the exhaustion in his voice. I felt bad that I couldn't be there to help out with the house and the dog and take some of the burden from him.

"I've got another big day tomorrow," he said. "I'm making a presentation about fire investigation to a class of new recruits at the Fire Department Training Center and I need to update my slides before I go to bed tonight."

It was disorienting to be talking about Mike's next day at work when in Japan it was already Friday night. "How about you?" Mike asked. "How's the case going?"

"Mediocre." I told him about traveling up to Fukushima and talking to Etsu Suzuki. "Maybe it's a lead, maybe not. It's scary to think that the yakuza could be involved in this."

"Be careful, Kimo. From what I've heard, the yakuza we have in Hawaii are nothing compared to the ones back in the mother country. This investigation could get very dangerous."

"I know. But we're going to leave the yakuza angle to Jutta Dore."

"How soon do you think you'll be able to come home?" I heard the longing in his voice and my own heart reacted to it.

I concentrated on not letting my voice crack as I said, "Maybe Monday or Tuesday. Ray and I are going to fly up to Hakodate on Hokkaido tomorrow, see if we can talk to the wife's family and friends and anybody else who knew them."

We said we loved each other, and I handed Ray back his phone.

He said he was going to call Julie, and I went down to the hotel gym to work out. It felt good to push my muscles, after so much inactivity—taking planes, trains and automobiles for the last couple of days. By the time I finished I was sweaty and achy.

Ray was melancholy when I returned. "What's the matter?" I asked.

"Vinnie's been crying for me."

"He'll survive," I said. "He's a tough little kid. Just like his dad."

Ray snorted, but at least he smiled.

While I was working out he had gone online and got us reservations the next morning for the hour-and-a-half flight to Hakodate. "I hope you don't mind," he said. "I booked us at a ryokan in Hakodate. It's a traditional Japanese inn and I'd like to try one."

"Sounds good to me. Any response from Salinas to our email?"

"Nope. He's probably asleep."

"If he sleeps," I said. "Could be that he's some kind of FBI robot, always programmed to wear dark suits and pressed white shirts."

"If that's the case, then we're getting programmed too."

"I work for the Bureau," I said. "I am not of the Bureau."

13 – Frightened Rabbit

The next morning, we rode the train out to the airport and checked in for the domestic flight. After takeoff, Ray turned to me, and it was obvious we'd had the same thing on our minds—the insertion of the yakuza into our case. "In the three years I've been in Hawaii, we've had maybe two or three cases with some kind of yakuza connection," he said. "Always small stuff. You think they could be branching out to terrorism?"

"I don't know," I said. "We've always thought of them as petty criminals, at least in the United States. Using Hawai'i as a way station between Japan and the mainland, smuggling methamphetamine into the U.S. and firearms back to Japan."

"And they control a lot of gambling and prostitution," Ray said.

"But nuclear arms? That seems a big jump."

As we circled for our descent, Ray leaned over my shoulder as we got our bearings. We were about to land on Hokkaido, the northernmost of the chain of islands. Like Pearl Harbor, Hakodate wrapped around a bay, with big container ships docked at an industrial port on the sheltered side. The mountain at the far end was surmounted by a series of telecom towers.

It was nearly twenty degrees colder in Hakodate than it had been in Tokyo, in the low thirties and damp. Before we left the terminal we both dug sweaters out of our bags and put them on under our coats. I added a scarf and a pair of gloves. The airport was a couple of miles out of town, and we took a taxi along an oceanfront highway. The area was not as crowded as Tokyo, without the frenetic pace of traffic and flashing neon signs.

We passed a sleek, modern streetcar in front of a simple Russian Orthodox Church with a single small onion dome, and I remembered we were close to Russia up there—at the same latitude as Vladivostok.

As we neared the ryokan the streets sloped down toward the harbor, and there was a thin frost of snow on roofs and trees. The ryokan was larger than I expected, three stories tall with a traditional arched roof over an entry court. At the front door, a middle-aged woman in a flowered kimono greeted us and asked us to remove our shoes. I was glad I had warm socks on because the stone floor was cold. That worried me; I like my creature comforts and I wasn't sure this ryokan was going to satisfy them.

She gave us each slippers and after checking us in, she led us down the hall. She opened the screen to a square room with traditional tatami mats on the floor. There were two simple ink brush drawings on the walls. The only piece of furniture was a single low table with a blanket on the floor and cushions around it.

"Where are the beds?" I whispered to Ray.

"The maids bring in futons in the evening," he said. "At least that's what the guidebook said."

The lady in the kimono bowed and left us in the room, closing the shoji screen behind her. There was a small bathroom adjacent to the room with a shower stall, sink and toilet. It was a far cry from the hotel where we'd stayed in Tokyo, much closer to the way I imagined Japanese people lived.

Had my grandfather grown up in a room like this? I wondered, as we pulled out the map of the city we'd printed back in Tokyo.

We had decided to begin with Chikako's sister, Ishi Kameda, a clerk at a store in Hakodate. We showed the address to the kimono lady at the front, and she said that it was down by the harbor, and that she'd call us a cab. We got back into our shoes by the front door, and I was able to make some small talk with the cabbie as we drove.

The cabbie dropped us in front of a series of brick warehouses across from a small yacht basin filled with sailboats. The address we had was a tourist-oriented shop with a front window filled with statues of round-faced cats with one paw raised. Each one wore a gold charm around its neck.

We stepped inside and the door jingled. A diminutive Japanese girl with a bright pink streak in her black hair approached us, and I recognized the resemblance to her sister—same oval face, same hooded eyes. Before I could say anything, though, she pointed at the cats in the window. "*Maneki neko*," she said. "Lucky cats. Great souvenir to take home. Bring good luck and prosperity."

She pointed at the cats in sequence. "White cat for happiness, black for safety." She rubbed her fingers together and said, "Gold for money, pink for love, green for students, red for children to stay healthy."

"Are you Ishi Kameda?" I asked.

She tilted her head sideways. "Yes?"

Since she appeared to speak some English, I introduced myself and Ray as police detectives from Hawai'i. "Chikako Kameda Griffin is your sister, right?"

She nodded sadly. "Yes, she died. My father, he say someone in Hawai'i tell him, from TV news."

"We're investigating the deaths of your sister and her family," I said. "We're both very sorry for your loss. We'd like to ask you some questions."

She looked around furtively, particularly at the older woman behind the register. "We go to tea shop, can talk there." She said something to the woman and then grabbed a puffy pink coat that matched her hair. She led us outside and down the street to a *kissaten*, a modern-style tea shop. We sat down at a table by the window.

A demure waitress in a formal kimono approached us and bowed, and we ordered *matcha* tea and *mochi*, rice cakes with different fillings.

"Were you and your sister close?" I asked after the waitress left.

"She two years older than me," Ishi said. "Growing up we are always together. But she much smarter, go to university, study English." She smiled weakly. "I work in my father's store. He always say I am stupid one, should marry rich man and have babies."

"Like Chikako?"

"Dale not rich, but he have big dreams," Ishi said. "My father think he is weak, can push him around."

The waitress returned with a steaming pot of tea and poured us each a small cup, then bowed and backed away.

"Push him around how?" I asked.

"My father is bad man. He do many bad things."

Her hands shook as she raised her teacup to her mouth. "Are you afraid of him?" I asked.

She nodded. "That woman in shop? I know she tell my father everything I do. When I don't make sales he yells at me." From the fear she demonstrated I believed he did something more than just yell at her.

She looked up at us. "You can tell me more about Chikako?" she asked. "How she die?"

Between Ray and I, we explained about the radioactive material found on the Usagi Maru, and how Chikako, Dale and their babies had died before they could reach port. Tears began to fall down Ishi's cheeks but she made no move to blot them.

"Is because of my father," she said, when the waitress had left. "He tell Dale he must make trip to U.S., carry something on his boat. He will give Dale lots of money when he make delivery. Chikako know it is something very dangerous but she won't tell me what. She say to protect me. She only agree with Dale because in U.S. she can protect babies from our father."

Ray and I both sipped our tea as we calculated the ramifications of what Ishi had said. That was the link we had been looking for. Chikako's father had arranged for Dale and Chikako to transport something very dangerous to the United States.

"Where can we find your father to talk to him?" I asked.

Ishi jumped up, knocking her chair behind her. The noise reverberated around the quiet tea room and the waitress stared at us.

"I say too much," Ishi said. "My father will be very angry. You cannot tell him you talk to me, please? He will hurt me."

"We won't tell him you spoke to us," I said.

"He will know. He know everything." From the way she held herself in, her front teeth over her lip, she resembled the little caricature on the bow of the Usagi Maru. And then, like a frightened rabbit, she dashed from the tea room.

"Should we go after her?" Ray asked, as the door banged behind her.

"I think she's told us all she can." I pulled my laptop from my backpack so I could take some notes, and started talking as I waited for it to warm up. "Akiro Suzuki stole something in a box with hazard markings from the Fukushima plant. Then he took what he stole to Nihonbashi, where the yakuza was helping earthquake and tsunami victims."

Ray picked up the thread. "Dore told us that a lot of men with yakuza connections work at the nuclear plants, so it's reasonable to assume Suzuki knew one of them. When he discovered he was dying, he made contact with someone from the yakuza and sold whatever was in the box to them, resulting in the big deposit in his bank account."

"Then he died," I said. "His wife said he had pancreatic cancer, and she thought it was a result of his work at the plant. Whether it was or not, he had reason to believe that his work was killing him, and he had a desire to leave his wife provided for."

"But the trail goes cold there," Ray said. "We can't be certain that the materials that ended up with the Griffins came from him. And they could only have been carrying part of what he stole."

I nodded, typing away. Then I looked up. "We've got this murky part in the middle—from Nihonbashi to Shiogama. How do we research that?"

"We have to talk to Chikako's father," Ray said. He looked through the information we'd been sent. "His name is Raiden Kameda. Maybe he feels guilty about what he did, and now he wants justice for his daughter."

I shook my head. "Anything he tells us is going to implicate himself in something very big and very politically dangerous. We need someone who knew what was going on but can't be implicated."

At the same time, we both said, "The mother."

I finished typing my notes and used the Wi-Fi card to send it to Salinas. Then I checked the file and found the address where Chikako's parents lived.

"There's no indication that the mother works," I said. "So seems like our best bet is to try the house and hope the father isn't there."

14 – Fences

. . . .

We hailed a cab and rode up into the hills around the city, stopping at an iron gate that surrounded what looked like a large property. We paid him, and I stepped up to the intercom.

After I pressed the button, and waited, a woman's voice said, "*Daredesu ka?*"

I answered in Japanese that I was a police officer investigating the death of Chikako Kameda Griffin, and the gate buzzed. I pushed it forward and Ray and I entered a sculpted Japanese garden. We walked down a pebbled path between stone lanterns, passing dwarf pines and lace leaf maples.

I knew, from something I'd studied long before in college, that we were in a *kaiyū-shiki-teien*, a promenade garden, where the visitor follows a path around the garden to see composed landscapes. Since it was winter, there was nothing in bloom and there was a sense of stiffness and rigor to the garden, each shrub manicured, no stone out of place.

We rounded a corner to a traditional wood-framed Japanese house, slightly raised above the ground with an open porch and curving tiled roofs. A beautiful woman in an elegant black kimono stood in the open doorway. She looked like a fifty-something version of her daughters—the same oval face and hooded eyes. Her hair was the same jet black as Chikako's.

We approached, and I bowed to her, then introduced Ray and myself. She bowed in return and invited us inside. We left our shoes and coats by the front door, and then she led us into the living room, where a brazier warmed the room. Silk paintings of reeds and cranes hung on the walls, and delicate porcelain vases filled the shelves of an glass cabinet. It was much more elegant than Mrs. Suzuki's simple apartment.

Mrs. Kameda invited us to sit on cushions around a low ebony table with intricately carved legs. This was the toughest part of an investigation for me, speaking with the families of the victims. Ray had a gentler touch than I did, so I often deferred to him. But the language barrier meant it was all on me—and I was afraid that my fumbling efforts at Japanese would insult Mrs. Kameda and prevent her from giving us any information.

"I have been expecting police ever since my husband and I heard that our daughter and grandchildren died." She paused. "Was it quick?" she asked, in a quiet voice. "They did not suffer, I hope."

"The doctor told us that Timmy and Tammy died quickly," I said. "I am sorry, the poison took longer for Chikako and Dale." I explained as best I could the way Dale had lovingly laid his wife and children in their beds. She pursed her lips tightly but did not cry.

"The Usagi Maru hit a bad storm," I said. "Dale wrote…" I paused, unsure of how to describe a logbook in Japanese. "The boat was damaged. A box they were carrying began to leak." I used the app on my phone to find the word for nuclear contamination and came up with "*Kaku osen.*"

She did not look surprised at the way in which the Griffins had died, which made me suspect she knew what was in that box.

She looked down at her wrist, where she wore an elegant diamond watch, which seemed incongruous with the spare look of the black kimono, then she stood up. "You must go now."

Ray opened his laptop and brought up the photos we had taken of Dale, Chikako and the children. "*Onegaishimasu,*" he said, and I was impressed that he pronounced the word for please so well. "Please help us."

I could see tears at the edges of her eyes. "It is too dangerous," she said. "Please, go. I will call a taxi for you, but you cannot stay here. There is a small store at the base of the hill. The taxi will meet you there."

She led us back out to the front door. "If you think of anything else we should know, we are staying at the ryokan by the harbor," I said, as she opened the door.

She didn't say anything, and we walked outside. It felt like the temperature had dropped significantly, and I huddled into Mike's coat. I wrapped my scarf around my mouth and leaned down into the wind as we walked back through the formal rock and pine garden.

"Whenever I see fences like this," Ray said, as we walked out through the gate, "I wonder if they are here to keep people out—or keep them in."

I thought about that as we walked back down the hill to meet our taxi. My heart broke for Mrs. Kameda, trapped in her beautiful home, and I worried that our trip to Hakodate would not provide the information we needed to bring justice to the deaths of her daughter and grandchildren.

There was no Wi-Fi at the ryokan, so we stopped at a café a few blocks away to go online. I checked my FBI and HPD emails first; there was a message from Emily Sukihara that Raiden Kameda was a yakuza oyabun, one of the most powerful in town. Probably would have been good information to have before we started the day. Salinas had received our emails and told us to keep looking.

I ended with my personal account, where I found an email from Mike. His presentation at the Fire Academy had gone well, but it was tiring to be "on" so much. He had taken Roby out for a long walk and was going to bed early. I looked at my watch and then did the calculations. He'd already be asleep back in Honolulu—the day before, as I kept reminding myself. So instead of calling Mike I sent him a long email.

I shared my frustration with the lack of progress in our investigation, my language difficulties, the reticence of Chikako's sister and mother to say anything against Raiden Kameda. By the time I finished I was thoroughly depressed.

Ray and I walked back to the ryokan in the gathering darkness, black birds swooping overhead and the cold wind blowing. As we approached the courtyard a taxi pulled up and Mrs. Kameda stepped out, wearing a long fur coat in shades of brown and tan and a matching fur hat.

"I cannot stay long," she said in Japanese. "But I have decided I must talk to you."

We led her inside, and the woman at the front desk helped Mrs. Kameda out of her beautiful coat. We left our coats and shoes in the lobby and the clerk led us into a side room where the three of us could talk in private. The room was much simpler than her own home, and I hoped that the surroundings would help her open up.

"My husband has brought me many benefits," Mrs. Kameda began in Japanese, as we sat on low cushions. "But also much pain. For many years I have tried to ignore that, but now that he has killed Chikako and her babies, I cannot look away anymore. For my daughter's spirit to rest, Raiden-san must answer for what he has done."

I translated for Ray, and then we waited for her to continue. Finally, she said, "My husband hears many things. Some provide him with business opportunities. A man he knew from Tokyo needed someone to carry these materials to the United States by boat. Raiden volunteered Dale. He thought Dale could make the trip by himself, but Dale said it was too difficult a trip for one person. He did not want to do this, but Raiden-san pressured him. Chikako, she wanted to go to Dale's country, to make a good life for the babies. And to slip away from her father and his power."

I quickly translated for Ray, then turned back to Mrs. Kameda. "Do you know who this man was?" I asked.

She nodded. "Of very high rank with the Yamaguchi-gumi."

The yakuza group that had been in Nihonbashi providing aid after the tsunami.

"Dale and Chikako sailed to Shiogama, and my husband flew there, to meet the person who carried the materials."

She grimaced. "My husband would not touch this box himself,

but forced my daughter to," she said. "For a man who calls himself strong he is very weak."

I didn't press Mrs. Kameda on her husband's illicit activities— that was up to the Japanese police to pursue. We needed to focus on tracing the box of plutonium. After I translated for Ray I turned back to her. "Do you know the name of this man from Tokyo?" I asked.

"Jiro Watanabe," she said. "He is very dangerous. When my husband learned that the boat crashed, he told me that he would have to leave for some time, until he could make amends with Watanabe. I could tell he was very frightened."

"Do you know where he went?"

She shook her head. "I have believed for some time he has another home with a mistress. Maybe he is there. Maybe he has gone farther."

She stood up. "Now, I must go. Even though he is not here, my husband knows what my daughter and I do, where we go and who we speak with. I believe it is time for Ishi and me to leave Hakodate as well. My husband has already sacrificed one daughter. I must make sure he does not do the same with her sister."

She left, and I told Ray the last of what she had said. "Lot of people have reason to be frightened," I said. "Mrs. Kameda and her daughter are scared of the father, and they're all scared of this yakuza guy in Tokyo."

We went up to our room to write down the notes of our meeting with Mrs. Kameda, then returned to the café for dinner. By the time we left, the night was cloudy and there were no stars to be seen. We took a shortcut through a narrow alley to get to the ryokan, and soon after we stepped into it we heard a car turn in behind us.

"There isn't enough room here for that car to pass us," Ray said. "We should have stuck to the street."

"We'll walk fast, and as long as we stay in the glow of the headlights, the car will have to follow us."

The driver of the car, though, didn't have the same idea, and gunned the engine over the alley's ruts. Ray must have realized as I did that the car was after us, and we both took off at a run. There was no place to go except forward; the backs of the buildings crowded right up against the alley.

The car's headlights were so bright I almost felt them searing into my back as it gained on us. As we dashed past a large beige trash can, I tugged the handle and toppled it into the alley behind us.

I heard the bang as the car plowed into the trash can and kept going. Just before the car caught up with us, I saw a place we could duck out of the way, and I grabbed Ray's arm and gasped, "To the right!"

15 – The Raw Prawn

Ray and I both dove against the back of a building that stopped two feet from the alley. I heard the roar of the engine and felt the rush of hot air as the car careened past us, then watched as it reached the street, turned right, and drove out of sight.

We remained flattened against the building for a moment, listening for the car, or the driver, to return. But the only sounds were distant traffic, no screech of brakes or car doors opening and closing.

"What the fuck was that about?" Ray asked, as he stepped back. "That car would have run us down if we hadn't jumped out of the way."

"Could it have been Raiden Kameda or someone who works for him?" I asked. "Mrs. Kameda said her husband always knew where she was going and what she was doing so he could have had someone follow her when she came to see us."

Ray shook his head. "Why run off like that, then?"

"It was a warning," I said. "To scare us off the case."

"Should we contact the local cops?"

"We'd have to tell them the whole story of going to see Mrs. Kameda," I said. "And we don't know what kind of connections Raiden has with the local police. We could be putting her in even more danger. What could they do, anyway? We didn't get a description of the car or the license plate number."

We ventured forward, all senses on alert. When we reached the street, there were no other pedestrians, just an intermittent flow of traffic.

We hurried to the ryokan. When I slid aside the shoji screen that led to our room, I had the immediate, visceral sense that someone had been in the room while we were gone, and it freaked me out. Then I recognized the pair of mattresses with sheets, coverlet and extra blankets. It was just the maid.

"I don't know about you, but I could go for a good long soak in the bath here," Ray said.

I shook out my shoulders and my arms. I could feel the tension in them. "Me, too."

After we'd cleaned up, the wizened attendant led us to the bath, where three Japanese men were already lounging. They nodded hello, and Ray and I both sunk naked into the warm water.

"So," I said, when we were settled. "What do we do next? It's not like we have a lot of other leads to follow here." I leaned back against the wall of the bath and let my legs float upward.

"We don't have any other names," Ray said. "All we have is the address of the marina where the Usagi Maru was docked when they were here. We could go over there tomorrow morning and see if we can find anyone who knew them. If we get nothing, we fly back to Tokyo tomorrow and meet with Dore on Monday morning."

"That works." I leaned my head back as two of the other men got up and left the bath, and another man joined us. I kept an eye on him for a minute or two to be sure he had no nefarious plans, but he appeared to be just another tired salaryman.

When we left the bath area, the ryokan's hallway felt frigid and I hurried ahead of Ray, eager to get warm again. I opened the shoji carefully but there was no evidence of danger, so I sat down beside the table, where the heater was. I gathered a blanket over me and Ray laughed.

"You really are a warm-weather kind of guy, aren't you?"

"I went to college in northern California," I said defensively. "It got cold there. Occasionally."

We were both tired, so after we warmed up we moved our mattresses close to the table and went to sleep, covered in blankets.

There were snow flurries the next morning, but by the time we finished breakfast the sky had cleared. Ray went to the café to look online for photos of Raiden Kameda, to see if perhaps we'd run across him without realizing it.

I walked over to the marina, huddled into Mike's coat and feeling a brisk wind against my cheeks. It was a lot like a yacht basin anywhere on a Sunday morning—sleepy sailors checking the rigging, smells of breakfast cooking, and the gentle rocking of the boats against the small waves.

Each boat I passed had its name painted in Japanese kanji on the stern, except for one that had been cutter-rigged like the Usagi Maru, with that extra sail. It was called The Raw Prawn and its home port was Melbourne, Australia. I hoped that whoever was on board spoke English, and might have known the Griffins.

I leaned across and rapped lightly on the hull. "Hello? Anyone home?"

A rangy white guy with a shaved head stepped out on deck. "G'day, mate," he said. He wore a T-shirt and tight running shorts, and just looking at him made me cold, even though I was wearing a coat, hat and gloves.

"Good morning," I said. "I'm looking for anybody who might know the Griffins, on the Usagi Maru."

He nodded. "A bad 'un, Dale is. You're a copper, aren't you? Good on you for looking into him." He smiled and said, "Want to come aboard? It's warm down below." He stuck his hand out. "I'm Kev."

I introduced myself, and stepped onto the boat, which rocked slightly. All the gear looked shipshape, but there was something louche about Kev that made my gaydar ping. He led me into the main salon and sat on the lounge, his T-shirt riding up a bit over his flat stomach. "Take your coat off and get comfortable," he said.

I looked around the cabin and I saw what looked like a Tom Bianchi photo of male nudes around a swimming pool. So my gaydar had been correct.

It was delightfully warm, and I was happy enough to shuck Mike's coat and the sweater I wore underneath it.

"Dale was a bludger, you know," Kev said, as I settled down across from him in my shirt and jeans. "A layabout, to you Yanks. Tried to get by doing as little as possible, and what he did was usually somewhere under the law."

"Dale ever get arrested?" I asked.

"Couple of times. But Chikako's dad has pull, always got the charges dropped."

I recalled Dore hadn't been able to pull up any criminal record in Japan for Dale Griffin. So that was why. "What kind of stuff did he get caught for?"

"Transporting stolen goods. Used to load up the Usagi Maru and ride along the coast, making pickups and deliveries for his father-in-law. He's not the only one—another bloke, Japanese, did the same kind of thing for him."

"You have his name?"

"Hiroto Endo. But you won't be able to talk to him. He left here the same time the Griffins did, both of them doing an errand for Raiden."

I pulled out my phone and started to tap in notes. When I finished, Kev cocked his head and looked at me. "They get caught, Dale and Chikako?" he asked.

"In a manner of speaking. They're dead, them and their two little babies."

For the first time Kev's joking manner dropped. "That's bloody awful," he said. "Chikako was a sweetheart and those babies were little angels. What happened to them?"

I gave him a brief version. "Did Dale ever say what he was carrying?"

He shook his head. "But whatever it was, Hiroto Endo had the other half of it."

"What do you mean?"

"Raiden came to me back in December, wanted me to go across the Pacific for him. He had some kind of material he needed to ship to the States, and he wanted two separate boats, each carrying one box. He'd already roped Dale into it."

He leaned back. "Not many boats here can manage it beyond the Raw Prawn—just the Usagi Maru and Hiroto's boat, *Kumo Nami*." He spelled it for me and I added it to my notes. "It means Wave Spider."

"You turned Raiden down?" I asked. "Was he angry?"

"Didn't matter to me. There was no way I was making such a long dangerous trip, no matter how much money he offered."

I tapped a couple more notes into my phone. There had been a second boat, with the other half of the plutonium. Where was it now?

When I looked up, Kev was grinning slyly at me. "You've got some Japanese in you, don't you?" he asked, letting his hand rest on his groin.

I'd been wondering what a guy like Kev was doing in a place like Hakodate. He was the type to be hanging around a beach in tight Speedos looking for man candy. But as he stared at me I realized why. "My Ojisan was from Tokushima," I said. "You like Japanese guys, don't you? That's what you're doing here."

"I'm an entrepreneur," he said. "I make connections for clients."

"Clients with yellow fever?"

He laughed. "You could call it that. Japanese boys are very open, very willing, especially if there's money involved. Lots of gay for pay, if you know what I mean."

"So you're a pimp," I said.

"What a nasty word." His other hand rested on the strip of taut flesh above his waist. "I prefer the term matchmaker." He sang a bit of the song from *Fiddler on the Roof*.

I was curious how someone like Kev could skate below the radar with such an operation. "Don't the police care about what you do?"

I asked.

"I have a good relationship with Raiden. I pay him a percentage of what I take in, and he and his connections on the police force make everything smooth for me."

Good thing Ray and I hadn't wasted our time going to the police about the car that chased us.

Kev was full of interesting information. I wondered what else he could tell me about Chikako's father. "What kind of guy is Raiden?"

"Tough as old boots. You don't get up to his position with the yakuza by being an old softie. Doesn't talk much. Usually I hand off my cash to one of his men." He leaned forward. "But the word on the street is that he's in trouble. Don't know why, but he's squeezing everybody who owes him money so he must be short somewhere."

So whoever had hired Raiden to get the plutonium to the United States already knew that one of the ships had been unable to fulfill its mission.

"Is he pressuring you, too?" I asked. "In person, or just through his men?"

"Haven't seen him in a while. One of the cops who works for him came by yesterday. But I'm not worried. If it gets too hot for me here, I just lift anchor and move on." He smiled. "Speaking of getting hot…" In a quick movement, he pulled off his T-shirt, exposing a flat, boyish chest. He was mostly hairless, except for a bit under his arms. "It is getting hot in here, isn't it? Must be all your sex appeal."

He ran his hand over his groin, and I could see his dick stiffening. "What do you say? Shall we have a go?"

He stood up and was about to drop his shorts when I said, "Thanks, but I have a partner back home."

"What he doesn't know won't hurt him." The shorts went down, and a very sizeable, uncut dick went up. "Come on. You know you want to."

I didn't, but my dick did, and that made me angry. I loved Mike and had no desire to cheat on him. And Kev wasn't even my type. He was ten years younger than I was, without the muscle or the body hair that usually turned me on.

"Nope, I don't." I stood up and grabbed my sweater, coat, hat and scarf.

"Hold on, Kimo. I didn't mean to scare you off. We could keep each other warm."

"I've got clothes to do that," I said, and I climbed out of the salon and out into the bitter air. I couldn't get my sweater on fast enough, so I just pulled on my coat, buttoning it up as I walked back down the wharf.

I was angry and chilled through by the time I got back to the ryokan. Ray wasn't back yet but the maid had already taken away the mattresses. I slumped down beside the table, trying to warm up from the brazier there. I wanted to get out of Hakodate, out of Japan. To be back home with Mike.

But feeling homesick was a waste of time. I ought to be flattered that Kev had thought I was cute enough to proposition. That hadn't happened to me for a while, maybe because I was getting older, or maybe because most of gay O'ahu knew that I had a boyfriend who was a muscular six-foot-four.

I thought back to what Kev had said. That Kameda was in financial trouble. That made sense; his daughter and son-in-law had lost a valuable cargo that had been entrusted to him. Someone, most likely the yakuza boss that Mrs. Kameda had mentioned, had paid Akiro Suzuki for plutonium that had been split into two boxes.

Raiden Kameda might have been paid to engineer the shipment, and at least one of the crews he had recruited, his daughter and son-in-law, had failed to make their delivery. Somebody was going to have to pay for that, and not just in cash.

Japanese put a huge stock in appearance, in doing what you promised. I'd read about the tradition of *yubitsume*, cutting off the tip of your left little finger as a form of penance or apology when you failed a mission. One of the ways we'd been trained to spot yakuza in the U.S. was the absence of this part of your finger.

Losing a shipment of this magnitude was a much larger offense.

Raiden Kameda would have to pay for the plutonium, as well as any lost profits to the Tokyo oyabun. Maybe the sacrifice of his daughter and grandchildren would be enough to offset the loss of face.

I opened my laptop and began typing a report on everything I'd learned from Kev. I went back to my phone and added my notes, including the information about the Wave Spider and the possibility it had been carrying plutonium, too.

When Ray returned from the café, he said, "My hunch didn't pay off. I found a booking picture of Raiden Kameda. He's an ugly mug, with a scar on his right cheek and a nose that looks like it was broken and badly set. I don't think we've seen him, and I'm tending to believe his wife when she said he took off."

"Or the yakuza got him before he could get out of town," I said. "I met with a guy at the marina who knows Kameda, knew Dale and Chikako too. He said that Kameda's a tough guy. And you have to be sharp to get to his position."

I turned my laptop to face him. "You ought to read this before we go any further. I got a lot of good information from the guy."

He read quickly through my report, asking questions, and I jumped in and clarified a couple of things. When we were finished, I said, "It's early Saturday evening in Honolulu. Can you raise Francisco Salinas on your phone? We need to get someone to track that boat ASAP."

Salinas answered his cell and I went through what I knew. "I'll email you the name of the boat and the captain," I said. "Can you find out if the Wave Spider has already landed in Seattle?"

"Will do. This is good work, guys. Let me rattle a few cages and get back to you."

After we hung up with Salinas, Ray said, "In looking up Kameda, I read some stuff that indicates your buddy Kev was right—Hakodate is notorious for yakuza infiltration of the police. While I was online I booked us on a flight back to Tokyo this afternoon. That all right with you?"

"Very all right with me," I said. "We don't want to end up in police custody on some trumped-up charge. And the longer we stay around the more vulnerable we are to whoever came after us last night."

16 – Royal Palace

We made it out of Hakodate without incident, and returned to the Hotel Okura by dinnertime on Sunday. Before we went out, though, Ray and I both used the hotel's Wi-Fi and his phone app to call home and check in.

"We might be able to fly home tomorrow," I told Mike. "Monday, for us. But I have no idea when that means we'll get back to Honolulu."

"That's good. I miss you, K-man." He paused for a moment. "You know what time it is here?"

"Sometime Saturday night?"

"Yup. You remember what we were planning for tonight?"

My dick stiffened. "I do. And I'll make it up to you when I get back. I promise."

"I'll hold you to that." We said we loved each other and hung up.

When we checked again after dinner, there was still no word from Salinas on the voyage of the Water Spider. We did some more searching online but neither of us could find anything useful. I was glad that we'd be able to get out of Japan soon, back to Honolulu where I had more sources and connections.

Monday morning we worked out again, then showed up at Jutta Dore's office at nine. As he ushered us in, I saw a big box of chocolates with a pink ribbon on his desk. He opened it and held it out to us. "Have a *giri-choco*," he said. "From my secretary. In Japan the women give gifts to men for Valentine's Day."

"Crap," Ray said. "I almost forgot. Have to send an e-card to Julie ASAP." I ought to do the same for Mike, with a big apology for not being home the night before.

"It's Sunday afternoon in Honolulu," Dore said, "so you've still got time."

We each picked out a chocolate. "You find anything out in Hakodate?" Dore asked, between bites.

We told him about our conversations with Ishi Kameda and her mother, and our suspicion that Raiden Kameda had orchestrated the scare in the alleyway, because we'd just spoken with his daughter and his wife that day.

"Anything else?"

"I talked to an Australian guy at the marina where the Usagi Maru used to dock," I said. As I repeated what Kev had told me, about the smuggling and Raiden Kameda's need for cash, he picked out another chocolate.

"Kevin Halloran?" he asked.

"I didn't get his last name," I said.

"The Japanese authorities have had an eye on Kev for a while," Dore said. "He's the man on the ground for a group that organizes sex tours for European men who like Japanese boys, but he's got some serious protection by the yakuza."

"He hinted at that business to me," I said. Ray looked at me, but didn't say anything. "Halloran said something else very interesting. It seems that someone broke the stolen plutonium into two separate shipments. The Griffins took one part, and a guy named Hiroto Endo took the other, in a boat called the Kumo Nami, or Wave Spider. Both of them were heading for Seattle. Francisco Salinas is trying to track that boat now."

"That's big news. You haven't heard back from him yet?"

"No. But like you said, it's the weekend back in the States so I imagine it takes time. Did you or the Japanese police make any progress on tracking the money that was paid to Akiro Suzuki?"

"Over the weekend the Japanese got the authority to poke into Kameda's bank account," he said. "And what do you know? He got a fifty-million yen deposit from the same account in the Caymans that paid Suzuki."

"So if we follow the money, it looks like there's a nexus," I said. "Someone with access to that Cayman Islands account paid both Suzuki and Kameda. Could that be the guy that Mrs. Kameda mentioned, Jiro Watanabe?"

"Quite possibly. Watanabe is a big shot with the Yamaguchi-gumi so it puts him in the right position. The Japanese are trying to get the Cayman government to give up the information on the account, but it's a tough road. And it doesn't get us any closer to the buyer in the U.S. But we do know that Kameda gave ten million yen to Dale Griffin, probably to finance the trip across the Pacific."

"If the Japanese do get access to the records of this Cayman Islands account, do you think there will be a transfer of cash from someone in the U.S.?" Ray asked.

"The yakuza are experts at covering their tracks," Dore said. "We may just find connections to other foreign accounts. It could take weeks to track them all backwards."

He leaned back in his chair. "Where do you go next? Back to Honolulu?"

"Do you think it's worthwhile for us to stick around?" I asked. "Look into this Jiro Watanabe?"

"I've got feelers out to a number of sources, from undercover agents with the Yamaguchi-gumi to organized crime detectives who are familiar with yakuza culture. Let them handle Watanabe." Dore stood up. "If you need any other help while you're in Tokyo, certainly call me. And if you hear anything about that boat headed for Seattle, I'd appreciate a heads up."

We thanked him and rode down to the lobby. "What aren't you telling me?" Ray asked as we walked outside and I pulled Mike's coat closer.

"About?"

"Kevin Halloran. I've worked with you a long time, Kimo. I can tell when you're holding back. There's more to your meeting with him than you told Dore, isn't there?"

"Halloran propositioned me. I told him no, and I left the boat. I didn't tell you because I didn't think it was relevant to the investigation."

"So you're not protecting him in any way?"

I looked at him. "Protecting a pimp? Why would I do that?"

"Because he was gay?"

"That's an insult, you know," I said. "I don't protect any criminals, no matter what they have in common with me." I took a deep breath. "I was embarrassed, all right? My dick wanted to have some fun with him, and that made me angry."

"Be flattered," Ray said. "The older we get, the less likely anyone's going to proposition either of us."

One of the many things I loved about Ray was the way my being gay made no difference to him—he treated me like just another guy.

"Let's find a café," he said. "See if we can get a flight home tonight."

There was another Doutor coffee shop a couple of blocks away, so we went inside, ordered our coffees and got online. While I checked emails, Ray found a site that would let us both send Valentine's e-cards.

The first email that popped up in my FBI account was from Francisco Salinas, a message that had been forwarded from the office in Seattle. The S/V Kumo Nami, piloted by Hiroto Endo, had arrived in at the Elliott Bay Marina in Seattle two days before and cleared Customs. Police had been dispatched but the boat was no longer at the marina and there was no indication of where it was headed.

Salinas's message ended with, "Fly to Seattle ASAP and liaise with local agents. Call me if you need anything."

"Guess what," I said to Ray, who looked up from his laptop.

"We're not going to Honolulu. Seattle, here we come. So much for celebrating Valentine's Day at home. At least I've been to Seattle before. And they speak English there."

I replied to Salinas's message as Ray looked for a flight. "There's a four-forty nonstop this afternoon out of Narita," he said. "We'll get into Seattle Monday morning around nine-thirty."

I added those details to my email. But before I clicked send I wanted to confirm I had it correct. "I'm still confused by all this day-changing stuff," I said. "It's Monday morning here, and if we get a flight this evening, we get to Seattle on Monday morning?"

"You got it."

We closed down our laptops and left the café. We were about a block from the hotel when Ray spotted a gift shop. "I'm going to duck in here and get a paper card for Julie," he said. "She'll love one in Japanese, and I can mail it from the airport in Seattle. I'll meet you back at the room."

"Sure." I walked ahead, but when I got to the hotel I decided I'd better go back and get a paper card for Mike, too. I turned around and saw Ray in front of the gift shop. Two big sumo-wrestler types were on either side of him, and it looked like they were trying to strong-arm him into a black car waiting at the curb.

The only word I could remember as I rushed toward them was *oukyuu*, which meant both 'emergency' and 'royal palace.' Whatever it was I was shouting, I hoped it would draw attention and keep those sumo wrestlers from getting away with my partner.

17 – We Get Around

Ray had some resources of his own, including a couple of years as a kid studying karate, and he managed to keep his captors occupied until I arrived to even the odds. I went right for one guy's nuts, grabbing and twisting, and he yelped and fell back. Ray kicked the other one and then the two of us took off for the Okura.

Sumo wrestlers are built for strength, not speed, and we got back to the hotel lobby before they could catch us. "Nothing like a kidnap attempt to get your blood flowing," Ray said.

"What was that all about?" I asked. "You think they were yakuza?"

"Didn't stop to ask. But who else would have a reason to go after one of us?"

He rubbed his right bicep. "You okay?" I asked.

"They twisted my arm. I'll survive."

A group of American tourists was waiting for the elevator, so Ray and I didn't say anything more until we were back in our room. "Why would someone want to kidnap one of us?" Ray asked. "Wouldn't that put more pressure on them? Create some kind of international incident?"

"It's possible that they didn't want to keep you, just rough you up enough to convince us to give up the investigation," I said. "Too bad they didn't know we were already on our way out."

It was almost noon, and we decided to forego any other sightseeing and head directly to Narita airport. Taxi fare, though, was going to be close to two hundred dollars for the two of us, and neither of us wanted to admit to the Bureau we were too scared to take public transport. We compromised on an airport limo for about thirty bucks each, where at least we'd be less vulnerable than on a public train.

We had the concierge arrange it, and rode on a comfy bus. I noticed that Ray was favoring his right arm and worried that he'd been hurt more than he was willing to say.

At Narita, we checked our luggage except for our backpacks, ate lunch, walked around for a while together, buying the Valentine's cards we needed, then sat down to use up the rest of the Wi-Fi minutes on our cards. We emailed Dore and Salinas about the abortive kidnap attempt on Ray, though we agreed that neither of us would mention it to Julie or Mike.

I wrote a long email to Mike about missing him and Roby, but also about how I'd felt in Japan—connected to my heritage while still feeling like an outsider. That maybe we should take a vacation to Italy sometime, track down where his father's family was from and see if he felt the same way.

I was still unsettled after I sent the message, so while Ray sat at the gate, I took a long walk through the terminal. I browsed aimlessly through the duty free shop, passed signs for a pod hotel, and shuddered as I passed an overwhelmingly yellow Pokémon store. I kept worrying about the attacks on Ray and me, going over everything that had happened, yet coming to no new conclusions.

Ray and I were seated far apart on the long flight, and I managed to sleep fitfully, though my dreams were restless and frightening. It was disorienting to arrive around ten o'clock in the morning and realize we had to go through Monday all over again. "Feels like that *Groundhog Day* movie," I grumbled, as we waited for our luggage to spin out on the carousel.

"Let's hope we don't have to repeat any of those attacks," Ray said. "I've had enough of being chased by a car and roughed up by fat dudes whose natural outfit is a diaper."

"How's your arm?"

He flexed it. "Still a little sore, but maybe I just slept funny."

I checked my watch and figured that it was close to eight AM in Honolulu. I called Mike. "I'm in Seattle," I said. "But at least you and I are on the same day of the week."

"Seattle doesn't get you home," Mike said. "I'm not sleeping well without you beside me. I keep worrying about you."

What was I going to say? Don't worry, I'll be fine? There had been two attempts to hurt Ray and me in Japan, and we were on the trail of someone violent enough to assemble the materials for a nuclear weapon. "Ray and I will look out for each other," I said. "You just take care of yourself."

"Julie was here yesterday," he said. "Vinnie was coughing up a storm and I told her to bring him here so my dad could look at him. She and I had a real heart-to-heart about being married to the FBI."

"And?"

"Neither of us are happy. We both think it's time you guys transferred back to HPD. At least you'll be home every night."

"I can't think about that right now," I said. "I'm in the middle of a case. We'll talk when I get back home."

"When do you think that's going to be?"

I felt a headache beginning to build at the back of my head. "I don't know, Mike. We just landed here and I still don't know what Salinas expects us to accomplish."

Ray nudged me. "Isn't that your bag?"

"I've gotta go," I said. "I'll call you later, okay? Still love me?"

"Of course. And Roby sends slobbery kisses."

I told him to kiss Roby back for me, and then grabbed my bag. Salinas's secretary had arranged a rental car for us, and while we waited in line I said, "So, Mike and Julie got together yesterday."

"Yeah, whatever Mike's dad did made Vinnie a lot better."

"Did she say anything about us leaving the FBI?"

He turned to face me. "No. Did Mike?"

"Yeah, apparently they talked about it. They want us home every night."

"I wouldn't mind that myself," Ray said. "It's been a good run with the Bureau. Interesting work. But I'm ready to go back to Homicide."

We stepped up to the counter and filled out the paperwork. It took us about a half hour to get to Seattle, mostly on the I-5 highway. Traffic was heavy so neither of us were eager to continue what was going to be a complicated conversation.

It took some maneuvering, and the map application on Ray's phone, before we reached the high-rise where the Bureau office was located. But at least all the signs were in English.

After we signed in, we were met by an agent named Frank Martinez, a stocky guy in his early thirties with cocoa-colored skin and a high and tight haircut.

"Here's what we know so far," he said, as we sat down in his office. "We have the police on the lookout for this boat, the ..." He looked down at the folder in front of him. "The Kumo Nami. It arrived at the Elliott Bay Marina here in town on Saturday morning. Call to the harbormaster came in at about zero-seven hundred, and an individual named Hiroto Endo went into the office and filled out the forms."

He turned to his computer and hit a couple of keys. "According to the Ships Stores Declaration, there are two men on board, Hiroto and Eiji Endo. They indicated that they planned to stay in the States for less than ninety days, and they reported no cargo other than their personal effects. Endo provided an outbound clearance from the port of Hakodate in Japan. The agent on duty cleared him at eleven forty-eight a.m."

"No one searched the ship?" I asked.

"ICE doesn't have the manpower to perform detailed searches on every boat that arrives from a foreign country, unless there's something suspicious. The boat remained docked at the marina until about nine o'clock yesterday morning, when it took off."

"Any indication where it was going?"

He shook his head. "No need for them to file anything if they're staying in the States."

The gloomy Seattle weather reflected our mood as Ray and I returned to our rental car. "What a waste of time, sending us here," Ray said. "We could have talked to Martinez on the phone and got as much as we did in person."

"We have to go where the action is," I said. "And right now we know that a shipment of plutonium landed here in Seattle. What was the name of that marina?"

"Elliott Bay." He pulled it up on his phone. "Looks huge. Not too far from here, but what can we do if we go up there? Look at the empty slip where the boat was docked?"

I knew how he felt—we'd uncovered a lot of information in Japan, but it hadn't moved our investigation forward very much. We knew where the plutonium had come from, who had moved it around Japan and how it had gotten onto the Usagi Maru and the Wave Spider. But we still didn't know who in the U.S. had ordered it and what its purpose was.

"What else can we do but check out the marina?" I asked. "If you've got a better idea, feel free to speak up."

"I'll get the directions," Ray said, and he turned to his phone. We left the city skyline behind us and drove north under the shadow of gray clouds heavy with rain, like big obsolete zeppelins moving slowly through the air. Elliott Drive paralleled the waterfront, and a huge cargo ship cruised slowly past us, heading in the opposite direction.

Our case was moving like that boat, though without the little tugboat to guide us. All we had was our intuition and the set of skills that had served us both through years as detectives.

I pulled up in the parking lot of a big round building and looked out at the rows and rows of sailboats. The marina was huge, much bigger than any in Honolulu, and I doubted a brief visit by a foreign sailor would caught anyone's attention.

At least I felt more grounded. Around us in the lot we saw a mix of ages and ethnicities, almost as much of a mix as back home. And they all spoke English.

We went to the harbormaster's office first, and verified the information that Special Agent Martinez had given us. We learned the number of the slip where the Kumo Nami had docked, and we walked down a long series of finger piers to reach it. The air was cool and damp, with a stiff breeze coming in from beyond the breakwater.

The sailboats around us ranged from single-handers to mega yachts, and I remembered the times Mike and I had gone out with Terri and Levi on his boat. My stomach ached with homesickness.

Another boat was already docked where the Kumo Nami had been. It was a transient area of the marina, near one of the outlets into the bay. The wind was particularly cold out there, blowing straight in from Puget Sound, and I missed the warmth and sun of O'ahu, where at least I could do something to solve a case.

We went up and down the pier, calling out greetings, knocking on hulls. Most of the boats were unoccupied, and the few sailors who were on board hadn't paid any attention to the Kumo Nami. We were discouraged by the time we'd checked with the last boat.

"This was a waste of time," Ray said, as the wind picked up and began shooting tiny pellets of rain at us. We hunkered down and hurried forward, and I slipped on the dock and if Ray hadn't grabbed my arm I would have ended up in the bay.

I was so busy regaining my balance that I didn't hear his yelp of pain, and it was only when we got back to the office, soaked to the skin, that I noticed he was favoring his right arm again.

We stood at a big plate glass window stared out at the storm. Our reflection showed that we both looked miserable. My hair was plastered down on my head and the sleeves of my windbreaker stuck to my arms like a second skin. Ray looked just as bad.

"There has to be a clue here," I said. "We haven't come all this way just to walk away empty-handed." I remembered going out on Levi's boat, and that there were always deckhands around to help us cast off and dock.

I turned around and walked back to the front desk. "Can you tell me which of your crew was on duty when the Kumo Nami came in?" I asked.

The clerk hit a couple of keys. "Manny. I can radio him for you."

He told us that we could find Manny out by the gas pumps. The rain had stopped as quickly as it had started, and we walked over there. A tall gray-haired man in a ball cap approached us carrying a mop and a bucket. "You're Manny?" I asked.

"Yup," he said. "You need something?"

Ray and I showed him our IDs. "You see a cutter-rigged sailboat from Japan that was here over the weekend?" I asked.

He nodded. "Helped them dock. Jerk didn't even say thank you."

"We're interested in a box that was on board," I said. "Hazard warnings on it. You see anything like that?"

He thought for a moment. "I saw a box," he said. "But they had a towel over it so I don't know what was in it." He held out his hands about two feet apart. "Yay big," he said.

"Where'd you see it?" Ray asked.

"Saturday evening I was getting ready to go off my shift when this guy came up to me, way over there." He pointed to another finger pier, far down the marina. "He asked me the way to a boat called the Wave Spider, and I had to look it up for him."

He pulled out his phone. "Have an app here that shows every boat that comes and goes. Otherwise we'd never be able to keep track of them. Fortunately the guy who registered had used both the Japanese and the English name. I walked him over here."

"Can you describe him?"

"Maybe fifty or so. Polo shirt, khakis, windbreaker, like most of the guys who sail out of here. He looked Japanese, or Korean or something, but didn't have any kind of accent." He stopped for a moment to spit out into the water, then wiped his mouth. "As I was walking away I heard the captain tried to speak Japanese to him, but the American guy didn't know the language."

Ray pulled out his phone and began to take notes.

"What about the box?" I asked.

"The two of them went below and I moved down the dock, untying some lines that had got tangled. Next time I looked up I saw the American guy climb off the boat, and then the captain handed him the box. He and another Japanese guy walked away, and that's the last I saw."

"Another Japanese-American?"

Manny shook his head. "I think he was crew. But I didn't notice him come back to the boat."

Ray looked up from his notes. "How about the boat? Anything more happen there?"

The man shook his head. "I work the second shift so I wasn't here when they left."

"Thanks," I said. "This is very helpful."

"These guys smugglers?" he asked.

"They're just part of an investigation." I handed him my card. "If you think of anything else, please give us a call."

He looked down at the card. "Honolulu?" he asked. "You come all the way over here for this?"

"We get around," I said.

18 – Blood Matters

I felt a whole lot better as we walked back up to the parking lot. Our trip to Elliott Bay had paid off after all. I was even starting to dry out.

"You think the guy Hiroto Endo met was a U.S. based yakuza?" Ray asked.

"I don't see it. You'd have to speak Japanese to be part of the yakuza, wouldn't you?"

Both our stomachs were grumbling, so Ray pulled up a list of restaurants in the area. We took clean, dry shirts in with us and changed in the men's room, and we ate a late lunch. "Good old American food," Ray said, as our hamburgers arrived.

"You won't get any argument from me."

As we ate, we walked through the movements of the Kumo Nami. "I wish we knew what this guy's plans are," I said. "Is he going to stay in the States? Head right back to Japan?"

"If I were him I'd get out of town," Ray said. "He's got to have recognized those symbols on the box and know that what he's doing is highly illegal. Now that he's dumped his cargo and most likely gotten the second half of his pay, he'll want to put as much mileage between him and Seattle as possible."

Martinez called as we were finishing lunch. "You got lucky," he said. "The boat stopped in at a marina in Port Townsend on its way to Canada, and the police have the captain detained and the boat impounded." He read out the address of the marina. "Let me know if you need anything."

"Can you run a check for any locals of Japanese origin who might be looking for nuclear material?" I asked. I gave him the name of the marina deckhand and Martinez said he'd follow up.

When I hung up something was still niggling at me. "Martinez said that the captain has been detained, but he didn't say anything about the crew. Wasn't there someone else on the boat?"

"A brother," Ray said. "Wonder what happened to him."

"We'll have to ask. Maybe he went off with whoever picked up the material."

It was early afternoon by then, and directions indicated it was about a two hour drive from Elliott Bay to Port Townsend, via a ferry from Seattle to Bainbridge Island and then a series of local roads.

"It feels like we're actually making progress," Ray said, as we drove to the ferry terminal in downtown Seattle. "All we have to do is pressure Hiroto Endo to tell us who he handed the plutonium off to."

"Easier said than done. If we're dealing with yakuza he probably won't want to give up the information so easily. And I sure as hell hope he speaks some English because I don't think it's going to be very easy to get a Japanese translator at the back of beyond."

Ray laughed. "My dad used to say that," he said. "Whenever we had to go somewhere far away—which to him was outside the Philadelphia city limits."

"My dad, too," I said. "Must be a dad thing."

"So Vinnie and your kids will grow up hearing us say it, too."

Thinking of Addie and Owen reminded me that I hadn't seen them since a week before Ray and I had left for Japan, and I missed them. They were at that stage where they were curious about everything, devouring books and asking millions of questions, and yet still young enough and small enough to cuddle up beside us, smelling of baby powder.

And that made me think of my conversation with Mike, and what Ray had said in the rental car line. "You want to go back to HPD,"

I said.

"I think I do. How about you?"

"Haven't really thought about it," I said. "I just figured that at some point the powers that be would say our time is up and send us back."

"And they have," Ray said. "Mike and Julie. The powers that matter to us."

"You do realize there's no guarantee we'll go back to the way things were," I said. "We could get sent to different districts, wherever the department needs us."

"It's worth starting the conversation," Ray said. "And HPD isn't our only option."

I had to navigate the ferry parking lot and get onto the tail end of the line for the 2:00 departure, so I had to let Ray's comment go for the moment.

It was a huge boat and it was cool to see how smoothly the whole process of driving on board and parking worked. We locked up the rental car and rode an elevator up to the upper level. The weather had cleared up a bit and I decided to stay out on the deck for a while. "I want to give Julie a call," Ray said, and headed inside.

I stood out in the sun and wind and spray and wished I was back in Honolulu. Eventually I couldn't help thinking about the future.

Did I want to go back to HPD? I'd gotten accustomed to working with the Bureau. The drive from our house in Aiea Heights out to headquarters in Kapolei was a reverse commute, and quicker and simpler than driving in to downtown Honolulu. I liked the challenge of investigating different cases.

If I returned to HPD and was lucky enough to be assigned to the Alapai Headquarters downtown, I'd be closer to my mom and the rest of my family. Mike's office at the Honolulu Fire Department was close by and we could go out together after work. I could go back to protecting and serving the people of Honolulu, as I'd wanted to do ever since I joined the police academy.

There was a downside, though, as I'd mentioned to Ray. HPD

employees worked at the discretion of the higher-ups, and Ray and I could be split up, one of us going to Wahiawa in the center of the island, the other out as far as Kahuku on the Windward Shore. We'd have to adjust to new partners, new teams and new bosses.

It might not even be our decision. We'd been assigned to the Bureau for nearly four years, which was a long rotation away from HPD. Any day we could get notice that we'd been reassigned.

The ferry ride ended too soon, and we got back in the car and continued up the tree-lined highway through the center of Bainbridge Island. It reminded me of the wilder parts of O'ahu, though the traces of snow through the forest made it clear we were in a much colder climate.

Neither of us spoke much as we drove. My mind was jumbled with thoughts of the future, of the approaching investigation, of the unfamiliar scenery. We crossed a trestle bridge over the Agate Passage and eventually approached a floating bridge over the Hood Canal at Port Gamble. "Are we getting close?" I asked Ray. My shoulders were starting to ache from hunching over the steering wheel.

"Another forty-five minutes. You want me to drive?"

"Yeah. And I'd love to stop for a minute, get something to drink and use the restroom."

"We'd better stop here then," he said. "The rest of the road looks pretty rural."

We parked at a local coffee shop, stretched, and fortified ourselves with caffeine. We discovered we were on the Kitsap Peninsula, and the clapboard buildings around us reminded me of New England— though I'd never been that far east in the States.

I picked up a tourist brochure and flipped through it once we were back on the road. As we approached the Hood Canal bridge, I said, "This is the world's longest floating saltwater bridge."

"Thanks for the travelogue," Ray said, peering forward at what looked like an approaching storm. "Remember when Julie and I first moved to Honolulu, and you used to point stuff out as we drove? You were like my built-in tour guide. I couldn't have acclimated as quickly as I did without your help."

"I was glad to get a partner who didn't fart all the time," I said, but I smiled. Ray and I had bonded quickly as detective partners and then as friends, and I couldn't imagine what the last nine years would have been like without him by my side.

The storm hit as we got to the bridge. Waves smashed against the supports and the wind pushed our rental car sideways. I grabbed the door handle and held on as the rental car rocked from side to side in the gusts. Ray turned the wipers on fast and clenched the steering wheel.

My eyes widened and I gasped involuntarily as the car skidded to the right, heading directly toward the guardrail. "Come on, you mother," Ray said, steering into the skid as we'd been taught, then turning the wheel back toward the center of the bridge.

It wasn't until we'd come to the end of the bridge that I realized I'd been holding my breath. I was glad I'd swapped places with him because I was afraid I was just too tired to have kept us on track the way Ray had. "Good driving," I said.

Ray shook out his right arm again as we made it into the shelter of the woods. Olympic National Park was to our left, and we were about as far west as we could get on the U.S. mainland. As we continued up the local road the storm passed us by, leaving the trees glistening in the late afternoon sunlight.

I could tell when we approached Port Townsend by the signs for wineries and bed-and-breakfast inns. And even though we had the heat on in the car, when a bank display showed the temperature as 46 degrees, I shivered.

We drove directly to the police station, a couple of blocks from the water, where Hiroto Endo was being held for interrogation. We went up to the front desk and showed our ID, and a detective named Dylan Hart came out to meet us.

Ray introduced us and mentioned that we were homicide detectives from Honolulu assigned to the Bureau's JTTF. That was a smart move, since I knew from our own experience that local cops often resented FBI involvement.

"You guys have kept us busy today," Hart said, as we followed him down a narrow hallway to an interview room. He was a blond in his forties with a pleasant, open face.

"The Special Agent who called said there might be radioactive material on board the boat, so I called in one of the state troopers who manages security at the port. He has one of those portable radiation detectors and he found traces of radioactive material on the Kumo Nami."

"That fits with what we're expecting," I said. "Has the captain said anything to you?"

"All he says is that he was on his way to Canada. His bad luck we caught up with him here. Port Townsend is the last stop before international waters," he said.

"Anything else?"

"Well, we had to get a search warrant in order to run the radiation detector, and fortunately the judge we work with gives us a lot of latitude in warrants. That's how we found the cash."

"Cash? How much?"

"Fifty thousand U.S. dollars," he said. "Stowed in a corner of the engine compartment."

"You guys are thorough," I said. "Good job."

"Yeah, we may be a backwater, but we've got some skills. You want to talk to Endo yourself? I can bring him in here. I'll even let you use our recording equipment if you want."

A few minutes later he brought in Hiroto Endo and set up a tape recorder for us to use. Endo was in his early thirties, slim and clean-shaven, wearing a T-shirt with the English words *Hello Titty* and a double-headed version of the Hello Kitty logo that looked like a pair of breasts.

I turned on the tape recorded, introduced myself and Ray and gave the date, time and location of our interview. "We are here to speak with Hiroto Endo, captain of the Kumo Nami," I said. I turned to him. "Do you speak English?"

"Little."

"Okay. We'll do our best to make ourselves understood."

I got him to verify the details of his departure from Hakodate, the trip across the Pacific and his arrival in Seattle. "You had one crew member?"

"Yes. My brother."

"Where is he now?"

He shrugged.

"I'm sorry, you have to speak for the recording," I said, and I repeated the question.

"Don't know."

"What do you mean, you don't know? Didn't he come across the Pacific with you?"

He shrugged again. I wanted to reach across the table and shake him. Didn't he know that what he and his brother had done could lead to the deaths of hundreds, maybe thousands of people? Did the words Hiroshima and Nagasaki mean nothing to him?

"Let's back up," Ray said. "Before you left Hakodate, someone asked you to bring something to the United States. Who was that?"

Endo's eyes shifted back and forth from Ray to me. "Yakuza man," he mumbled.

"What was his name?"

He wouldn't say. It took a long time to convince him that we already knew who had paid him, that we were investigating that man and would arrest him before he could do anything to hurt Endo.

He finally admitted that Raiden Kameda had hired and paid him. He swore up and down that he didn't know what was in the box. He admitted that he recognized the hazard symbols, but said Kameda told him the marks were just for show, nothing to worry about.

"Do you know Dale and Chikako Griffin?" Ray asked.

Endo nodded, then said, "Yes, they stay at same marina."

He admitted he'd known the shipment was split between him and the Griffins. He had taken a slightly different tack than Dale had, so he'd avoided the storm that had knocked them off course.

"Did you get a bonus for getting to Seattle first?" Ray asked.

"No. Just regular money. Police take money. They will give it back? Is mine?"

"Who gave you the money?" I asked. "Another Japanese?"

Endo laughed harshly. "He not even speak language. American man."

"What's his name?"

Endo shrugged again. "He never say."

"But you had to have some way to get hold of him," I said. "How did you make arrangements to meet him?"

"Email. Through radio. When I am one week from Seattle, then three days, then one day. He meet me at marina in Seattle."

He gave me the address he'd used, and I made a note of it.

"When this guy showed up, how did you know he was the man you were emailing?" Ray asked.

Endo looked at him like he was stupid. "Because he have money."

"Where's your brother, Hiroto? Did your brother go off with the man who gave you the money?"

I could tell from the way he wouldn't meet my eyes that he was hiding something. "Did this man promise to hurt your brother if you said anything?"

He looked at me, his eyes wide. "No, he promise to help."

It took a while, but he eventually admitted that his brother had run into trouble with the Japanese authorities, and Hiroto had brought him to the U.S. so he could get a fresh start. The man with the money had promised to take his brother back to where he lived, help him get a job and get papers to stay in the States.

"So where's your brother now?"

"Don't know. He say he will send me email when he get to Idaho."

He realized he'd said too much. "No, I say wrong place."

I shook my head. "No, you just didn't mean to say it. Your brother went with this man to Idaho. A man whose name you don't even know."

He started to cry. "Is my brother," he said. "I take care of him."

I looked at Hiroto Endo. If I were in his shoes, I'd do the same thing, even though I had sworn an oath to uphold the law of the United States. Sometimes blood matters more than anything else.

19 – Chasing the Goose

No matter what else we asked, Hiroto Endo had nothing more to say. We ended the interview and had Dylan Hart take him back to his holding cell. The email address Endo had given us was a generic free one, and I knew it would take a lot of paperwork to get any information on it from the host, but I sent it to Tomlinson anyway in case he could get something out of it.

Ray and I stayed in the interview room, composing a report on what we'd learned for Francisco Salinas.

"Endo said that his brother went off with whoever picked up the box of plutonium," I said. "How can we track him?"

"Won't be easy, if he's riding in a private vehicle," Ray said. "Though we don't know for certain that Endo's brother was going all the way to Idaho. Maybe the guy just gave him a ride to a bus depot or train station."

I emailed Jutta Dore and asked him to get hold of Eiji Endo's mug shot from the Japanese police. "We can send the photo to the local police between here and Idaho," I said, when I finished.

Then I looked at Ray. "Didn't we find some terrorist connections in Idaho?" I looked back through all the notes we'd taken, and I felt my exhaustion setting in. "Here it is. We came up with a couple of possibilities."

I'd focused on Art Duncan, a former nuclear engineer who lived at a compound outside Boise with a group of like-minded followers. Ray had come up with Brian Kurokawa, an animal rights activist. "Kurokawa is a Nisei," I said. "So he could fit the bill of a guy who looks Japanese but doesn't speak the language."

"True. But we can't eliminate Duncan. He could have sent one of his lackeys to pick up the plutonium."

I emailed Ryan Tomlinson, the valley-guy speaker from the High-Tech Intelligence Task Force, and asked him to put together a photo array including pictures of Brian Kurokawa and any Japanese-Americans who followed either him or Duncan. Hiroto Endo wasn't going anywhere, and we could come back the next morning and show him the array, see if he could identify the man his brother had gone off with.

By the time we were finished darkness had fallen and both of us were exhausted. Detective Hart recommended a bed-and-breakfast for us in an old Victorian house a few blocks away, and we drove over there.

A sixty-something woman with flowing shoulder-length gray hair met us at the door. "Welcome to the House of Aquarius," she said. "I'm Starshine. Come on in."

It felt like stepping into the 1960s. Starshine wore a batik T-shirt and faded jeans, bangle bracelets, and silver rings on each finger. The photos on the walls around us were of Haight-Ashbury, the Summer of Love, and hippies holding up two fingers and posters that read "Death to the Pigs!"

My blood pressure rose. "I don't think this is the right place. Sorry to bother you."

Ray looked at me. "This is the place Detective Hart sent us."

I nodded toward the wall, and Starshine saw what I was looking at. "Oh, don't mind the pictures," she said. "Those are old history. If I didn't like cops I wouldn't have let Dylan go to the police academy."

"Detective Hart is your son?" I asked.

"You're surprised? You should meet his sister. Saffron got her MBA at Stanford and runs a venture capital firm in Silicon Valley. See what lengths kids will go to get away from their old hippie parents?"

She smiled again. "Now, you look like you could do with a rest. I've got a room on the second floor for you."

She turned to lead us upstairs and I looked at Ray, who grinned back at me. "Imagine what Addie and Owen and Vinnie are going to do to get back at us."

"You two have kids?" she asked.

"My wife and I have a five-year-old boy," Ray said. "He's a handful."

"And my partner and I have four-year-old twins," I said. "They live with their moms most of the time but we see them all the time."

I wasn't usually so forthcoming about the situation with my kids, but I had the sense that Starshine wouldn't mind at all.

The room had two double beds and a big window that looked out toward the ocean. "Breakfast is from eight to ten," Starshine said. "Washer and dryer in the mud room on the first floor—two dollars a load."

After Starshine left, I flopped on one of the beds. "I'm beat," I said.

"So am I. But I'm almost out of clean clothes. Why don't we put a load in the washer and then get something to eat?"

We carried our dirty clothes downstairs, where we met Starshine's husband, Moonglow. "But you can call me Moon," he said. He looked a lot like his son—the same square build and blond hair, though shading more toward white. He recommended a restaurant only a couple of blocks away, and Ray and I walked there. The air was cold and damp even beneath Mike's coat, his scarf and gloves.

"Starshine and Moonglow," Ray said. "You think they chose those names after they met? Or that they hooked up just because their names matched?"

"I can't even begin to guess," I said. "Imagine growing up with them as your parents."

We laughed and speculated on how our kids would grow up to rebel against us, and after a couple of glasses of the local Syrah wine, I began to relax. We ordered locally harvested pan-fried oysters and pasta with mushrooms that had been growing in the woods only the day before. It was excellent, and the combination of food, wine and exhaustion knocked us both out.

We staggered back to the bed and breakfast and collapsed into bed, but just before I went to sleep I texted Mike to say where I was, and added a couple of heart emoticons.

The next morning we woke to an email from Tomlinson with a photo array and another from Dore with a photo of Eiji Endo. After a breakfast of orange juice and Starshine's homemade blueberry muffins, we packed up. "Are you going by the police station?" Starshine asked as we paid her for the night's lodging.

When we said yes, she gave us a basket of muffins to deliver to her son and his colleagues. "You ever think about living in a place like this?" Ray asked, as we drove the few blocks to the police station. "Small town, know your neighbors?"

"O'ahu is enough of a small town for me," I said. "Yeah, it's charming here but it's kind of like a theme park. Not real enough."

"I bet they have real world problems here, too," Ray said.

The desk sergeant was delighted with the basket of muffins, and let us use her computer to print the photo array Tomlinson had put together for us. Then she brought Hiroto Endo to the interview room, and he didn't hesitate—he fingered Brian Kurokawa as the man who'd paid him.

"You let me go now?" he asked.

I shook my head. "Not our call to make. You smuggled nuclear materials into the United States. My guess is you'll be transferred to Federal custody soon and then you'll have to see how things play out."

After Endo returned to the holding cell, Ray and I put together another quick report. There were no vehicles registered to Brian Kurokawa, and Endo hadn't seen what he was driving, so we couldn't put out a BOLO on his plates. Detective Hart said he'd send out the photo of Eiji Endo to the Washington State Police. "Most logical route is to take I-90 east," he said, showing us the highway on a map. "I'll notify the local departments along the way, too."

He also agreed to monitor the email address Hiroto Endo used in case Endo's brother emailed him to say where he was. And that was about all we could do in Port Townsend.

We shot a report off to Salinas. "Still too early to call Honolulu," I said, looking at the clock. "What do we do now?"

"Might as well head back to Seattle," Ray said. "With luck, we'll be able to get a flight to Honolulu tonight. Imagine that. Sleep in my own bed with my wife. Who doesn't snore."

"I don't snore," I said. "Mike would have told me if I did."

"Mike loves you," Ray said.

"And you don't?"

Ray just snorted.

Cell service went in and out as we drove, so I couldn't call Mike until we got to the Bainbridge Island, where we had an hour to kill before the next ferry to Seattle. We found a nearby coffee shop, and after we placed our orders I called Mike.

"Not too early for you, is it?" I asked, when he answered, sounding groggy. "I keep getting screwed up with the time differences."

"Have you forgotten Roby?" he asked. "And his desperate need to go out and relieve himself at the crack of dawn?"

"Who is Dawn and why is he reliving himself on her crack?" I asked.

"Very funny. I'll book you in at the comedy club for a special engagement if you ever get home. Where are you today?"

"An island across some water from Seattle," I said. "Waiting for a ferry back there." I explained what we'd been doing.

"So does that mean you can come home?" he asked.

"It's up to Salinas," I said. "He's the second call on my list this morning."

"Glad to hear I still rank first," Mike grumbled. "You're staying safe, aren't you?"

"Of course. Last night we stayed at this bed and breakfast run by a pair of old hippies, Starshine and Moonglow." I told him about the décor, and the way that the couple's kids had rebelled against them, and we laughed until my cell pinged with an incoming call from Salinas.

I told Mike I loved him and switched over to the other call. "Got all your information," he said. "Good work. We're closing in on this guy. Where are you now?"

"On our way back to Seattle," I said. "We want to get a flight out this evening and come into the office tomorrow."

"No, I want you to stay on this guy's trail. Head to Idaho."

"Idaho?" I asked, and I felt my voice go funny.

"One of the fifty states," Salinas said. "I'm sure you're familiar with it."

Everybody was a comedian that morning. "Already notified the police in Idaho Falls to pick up Kurokawa for questioning, but no one is at his home," Salinas said. "They have the property under surveillance in case he returns."

"So you want us to fly all the way to Idaho Falls and Kurokawa isn't even there?"

"It's our best bet," Salinas said. "If he shows up, you'll be there. If he doesn't, at least you can investigate him, see what kind of operation he has there."

I was not happy. I'd been looking forward to heading back to Honolulu, not continuing what was turning out to be a wild goose chase. But we worked at his direction, and if Salinas wanted us in Idaho Falls, we'd go there.

I told him we'd get on it, hung up, and relayed the message to Ray. "You can't blame the guy," he said. "If Kurokawa is taking that plutonium to Idaho we need to get there as soon as possible and intercept him before he can use it."

"If he's the one who picked up the plutonium, which is still unconfirmed, by the way," I said. "Then he'd have to drive, because you can't take plutonium in your carry-on bags."

"Or check it."

Ray looked at Google Maps, which indicated that it was about a twelve-hour drive from Seattle to Idaho Falls, close to the Montana border, and some snow in the high mountain passes might have made the trip even longer. It was a shame we had no information about the kind of vehicle he could be driving so we couldn't alert highway patrols along the way.

"If we go direct to the Seattle airport we can catch a flight to Salt Lake City that connects to one to Idaho Falls and gets in this evening."

"No direct flights to Idaho Falls?"

"Nope. There are plenty of flights from Seattle to Boise, but no airline flies between there and Idaho Falls. It's a four-hour drive so we'll actually get there faster by heading to Utah first."

"Time is of the essence," I said. "We don't know what he's planning to use the plutonium for, but we've got to assume he'll be ready for it as soon as he gets to Idaho Falls."

We got back on the ferry and I used the down time to call my mother. I remembered that my dad's mother had grown up in Idaho Falls. Maybe there'd be some trace of her or her family still there. As long as I'd gotten in touch with my Ojisan's heritage when I was in Japan, why not look into Granny, too?

"You're going to Idaho?" my mother said, after I'd explained. "I thought you were in Seattle."

"We are. But they have these things called planes, Mom. They can take you from state to state, even country to country."

"No need to get snippy," my mother said. "Remember what your father said."

"I brought you into this world and I can take you out of it, too," I said. "Yeah, right, Mom. So tell me about Idaho Falls. We have any family still there?"

"I'll have to log in to the Mormon database," she said. "They're saving all our souls, you know. Tracing everyone's dead relatives so that they can be blessed and allowed into heaven."

"Dad grew up Mormon, didn't he?" I asked.

"If you can call it that. After your granny's first husband died, the missionary she came out to Hawai'i with, she met your grandpa through the Mormon stake in Honolulu. But I don't think either of them had the taste for it."

"What do you mean?"

"Back then, if you weren't white they considered you some kind of savage and not fit for full church membership, and they didn't have very enlightened attitudes toward women, either. By the time I met your father none of them were going to the Mormon church."

"I remember Dad took us to the big church in Laie once," I said. "Lui was maybe eighteen or nineteen and he was interested in the whole missionary thing."

"Your father indulged you all too much," she said. "If you recall I didn't go with you. Just you boys and your father."

As we got farther from land the cell service was getting worse, so I told my mother I'd call her later. I stood on the ferry deck and tried to remember that service, but I was just a kid and I hadn't paid much attention. I did recall being surprised that my father was so familiar with the service. He even spoke to someone he'd known as a boy. It was a whole different side to him, seeing him dressed up in a shirt and tie, and the way he knew the hymns by heart.

Had I missed out on something by not being raised within an organized religion? Mike was Catholic, though not very observant. Harry had grown up in the Chinese church, and Terri and her family had been active members of the Kawaiaha'o Church, where my family and I had gone occasionally for holidays. I'd gone to Hawaiian school for years, learning not only the language and the culture, but also stories of the ancient gods, and I'd always thought that was enough religion in my life.

What about Addie and Owen? At Mike's request, the twins had been christened at St. Filomena's, the Catholic church his parents attended, but we hadn't taken their religious instruction any farther than that. Did I want them raised as Catholics? In some other faith? Did it matter to me?

The ferry docked, and Ray and I got back into the rental car and waited to exit. "I'm still having trouble wrapping my head around an animal rights activist needing plutonium," I said, as we crept forward. "What if we're on the wrong track completely, and some other guy with Asian features picked up the stuff from Endo?"

"Then we get to Idaho Falls, find Kurokawa, and establish he's not involved. Remember, we're not the only ones on this case. There are agents all over the place trying to figure out what's going on. We're just one cog in a giant wheel."

"Is that supposed to make me feel better?"

"No. It's supposed to get your head out of your ass so we can focus on the task we have. Which is to find Brian Kurokawa as soon as possible."

While we waited for our flight, I checked my email and found a message from my mom, with a PDF attachment of a family tree. "The only one of your granny's siblings who stayed in Idaho Falls was her youngest brother, Absalom," my mother wrote. "A woman named Kim Carhartt uploaded her part of the family tree about a year ago. There's an email feature inside the program and I contacted her and let her know you're coming to Idaho Falls and would like to talk to her. I gave her your email address."

I hadn't expected to meet a cousin but perhaps that would give me a way to kill time while Ray and I waited around in Idaho Falls to see if Brian Kurokawa showed up.

According to the family tree, my granny, Sarah Carhartt, was born in 1915. Her brother Absalom had been born seven years later. Kim Carhartt was his granddaughter, born in 1970, which made her four years older than I was. According to the tree, at least, she was not married and had no children.

They called boarding for our flight to Salt Lake City, and I didn't check my email again until we had landed in Idaho Falls on Tuesday evening. A message from Salinas indicated that there had been no sighting of Kurokawa yet.

I scanned through the rest of my mail, deleting the junk, and found a message titled "From the LDS Genealogy Archive." I opened it.

"Hi, it's funny that your name is Kimo and mine is Kim. Guess we must really be cousins, LOL! Your mom says you are coming to Idaho Falls. Would love to meet you and talk about family."

She included her phone number and her email address. She said she was an Idaho Conservation Officer so her schedule was flexible, and if I let her know where I was and when I was available she could make arrangements to meet me.

I had no idea what a conservation officer was, so I Googled it. I discovered that she was an officer who enforced wildlife laws, which was a pretty cool police job.

I called her number and introduced myself. "Hey, it's so cool to hear from you," she said. "When did you get into town?"

I looked at my watch. "About twenty minutes ago," I said. "Still waiting for my luggage to come around the carousel. Assuming it followed me here from Seattle."

"You must be starved. Why don't you come over here for dinner?"

"I couldn't impose on you," I said. "And besides, I'm traveling with my partner."

"I insist. I caught a couple of trout today and we're just about to start cooking them. There'll be plenty for all of us."

I gave in. At least we'd get some information from someone on the ground, and I was curious to meet this distant cousin whose name was so close to mine.

20 – Proceed With Caution

When we walked out to where the rental cars were parked tiny flurries of snow swooped around us. I stuck my tongue out to catch one and was startled at how cold it was. Ray and I checked in at a chain hotel near the airport, then followed Kim's directions to her house, a bungalow with a fieldstone foundation and dark-green shutters.

"You're sure she's okay with me tagging along," Ray said, as we walked up to the porch, where a pair of Adirondack chairs huddled against the wall, waiting for spring.

"She's a cop. I'm sure we'll all be fine."

When Kim came to the door I was surprised that she looked more than a little like me—down to the slim build, short black hair, and the epicanthic fold over her eyes. "Oh my god," she said. "We could be twins."

She hugged me, then said, "Come on inside. It's cold as a witch's tit out there."

The wood-paneled inside of her house reminded me of a wilderness lodge. A peeling canoe paddle was hung on one wall, along with photos of mountain streams and wild animals.

A chunky woman with multiple piercings came out of the kitchen. "This is my girlfriend Cindy," she said. "And this is my cousin Kimo and his partner…"

"Ray Donne," Ray said.

Kim must have noticed Ray's wedding band, because she asked, "Are you guys married?"

I realized what they were thinking. "Ray and I have worked together for so long we might as well be married," I said. "First at the Honolulu PD, now the FBI. His wife and my boyfriend get jealous sometimes."

"Dinner's almost ready," Cindy said. "Everybody come to the table."

I felt immediately comfortable with Kim and Cindy, and I wondered if it was because they were lesbians, or because Kim and I were cousins and there was some deep family tie between us.

As we ate, Kim told us she'd spent the day with a biologist, collecting water samples from trout streams. "He wanted to inspect some trout, too, so I got to catch them. And keep them, of course."

"Lucky us. The trout's delicious."

"That's all on Cindy. She's the chef in the family. I'm just the hunter-gatherer."

We learned that Cindy was a computer guru who worked from their house, that they'd been together six years, and that they had a menagerie of wounded and rehabilitated animals in a small structure out back.

"Kimo said you were a cop, too, Kim," Ray said.

"We enforce wildlife law," Kim said. "Check for permits, make sure folks aren't hunting or fishing out of season. But a big part of our job is conservation-based. We trap, tag and transplant wildlife, and work with landowners to resolve wildlife damage problems."

"Sounds much more relaxed than investigating homicides," I said.

"It's similar in many ways," Kim said. "We collect the same kind of evidence—ballistics, DNA, hair and blood. And we like to say that the real victims are the residents of the state of Idaho, because the animals belong to all of us."

"You'd be surprised at the wackos we have here," Cindy said. "Tell them about the survivalists who were polluting that stream."

We turned to Kim.

"This guy and his family moved out here from Chicago," she said.

"They built a cabin up in the woods on a stream that feeds into the Snake River, with an outhouse. They felt they were exercising their God-given right to poop into the river. Willing to defend that right with a whole range of weapons, too."

"Wow. How do you handle something like that?" Ray asked.

"Very delicately. With lots of scientific evidence that showed that by eating the fish in the stream, they were eating their own poop again. The wife was grossed out by that so they agreed to put in a composting toilet. No more pollution, and they got all-natural compost to use in their garden."

Over slices of chocolate cake Cindy had baked, we talked about our case. "The guy's name is Brian Kurokawa," I said. "You ever heard of him?"

"Not that I can recall. But my mom knows every Japanese person in the state or knows someone who does, so I'll check with her and let you know."

"Your mom's Japanese?" I asked.

She nodded. "My dad went to Japan for his mission. Met my mom, converted her to LDS and brought her back here."

We talked about our family tree, and I could see both Ray and Cindy were getting bored with hearing about siblings and cousins, and I was feeling beat anyway, so we thanked Cindy and Kim for the meal and went back to the motel.

Ray wanted to call Julie, and to give him some privacy I took my cell down to the motel lobby and called Mike from in front of the electric fireplace. "We're in Idaho Falls," I said.

"Where the hell is that?" he asked. I heard Roby barking in the background.

"Just east of Craters of the Moon," I said. I'd seen the signs for that national park when we got off the plane. "Not too far west of the Montana border." I told him about meeting Kim and Cindy, how weird it was to meet blood kin I'd never known and feel immediately connected.

"I thought you were coming home from Seattle." Roby was still barking.

"No, I told you I had to wait to hear from Salinas."

He turned away from the phone to tell Roby to shut up. "The dog misses you," he said to me, when he came back. "He's getting cranky."

So are you, I wanted to say, but I refrained. "Sorry, sweetheart. I miss you too and I promise I'll come home as soon as I can."

It took a few more minutes of reassurance before I could end the call. By the time I got back to the room Ray had finished speaking with Julie and he was just as depressed as I was.

Wednesday morning we woke to a blanket of snow covering the motel parking lot and all the cars. "Wow," I said, as I looked out the window. "I've never seen that much snow in one place before."

"Not even on top of Haleakala?" Ray asked.

"I've only been up to the summit a couple of times, always to bike down, so we've gone when it's warmer."

A man in the parking lot was scraping the snow off his car, and beside him a little boy was laying in the snow. "Holy crap. Look at that. Is that kid dead?"

Ray hurried to join me at the window. "He's not dead, he's making a snow angel," he said. "Look—his arms and legs are moving."

A moment later the kid jumped up, and in the snow I could see an outline that looked a bit like an angel. "Did you do that when you were a kid?" I asked.

"Of course. And made snowmen and had snowball fights. While you were swimming and surfing."

"I'll take my childhood," I said.

We loaded up on croissants, muffins and orange juice at the continental breakfast in the hotel lobby, listening to other travelers complain about the snow and driving conditions.

"So what do we do today?" I asked. "We don't have any leads to follow."

"We do what we'd do if we were in Honolulu," Ray said. "We hit the street. If the guy lives here, he has to buy groceries, get his hair cut, whatever. We keep talking to people until we find someone who knows him."

The motel had a small business center—two computers and a printer in a glassed-in room. We left one of them free for people who needed to print boarding passes and used the other to look for photos of Brian Kurokawa we could show around town.

We found several booking shots from the times he'd been arrested. He'd chained himself to trees, sabotaged logging sites by scattering nails on access roads, and thrown rotten tomatoes at a state senate session.

But those kind of pictures have a tendency to prejudice witnesses—something about the flat background was a giveaway, and that made people think the person was already guilty of something. So we kept looking, and found a couple of good pictures from several different animal rights websites. There, he was lauded as a hero for his efforts to protect the habitats of the spotted bat, the cliff chipmunk, and the flammulated owl.

The second computer freed up, and while Ray put together a list of what we already knew about Kurokawa, I pasted his photo into Google's image search to see where else I could find him that he might not be identified by name.

I was surprised at how many places I found his face, often in group shots of environmental activists. The one that jumped out at me, though, was on the website for the Nuclear Protection Organization—the group run by Art Duncan, the former nuclear scientist who now advocated using weapons of mass destruction against United States enemies.

Brian stood beside Duncan, a man in his fifties with a scruffy beard and military-short brown hair. Duncan wore a T-shirt that read "If I charge, follow me. If I retreat, kill me. If I die, avenge me."

Kurokawa wasn't listed by name in the photo, which is why he hadn't shown up in my initial search. The brief squib that accompanied the photo read, "NPO leadership meets with allies in environmental protection," and made vague promises of plans to work together.

"Look at this," I said, showing the screen to Ray. "Duncan's the guy who used to work at the Lawrence Livermore labs. So he'd know what to do with plutonium."

"And he might have delegated Kurokawa to pick up the shipment because he assumed Kurokawa spoke Japanese."

I nodded, then went back to our notes to check on Duncan's location. We had an address for him in a small town called Eagan's Gap, Idaho, and a quick look at the map showed it was along the South Fork of the Coeur d'Alene River, about halfway between Coeur d'Alene, Idaho and Spokane, Washington.

"We're closing in on him," I said. "It looks more and more reasonable that Kurokawa is the guy who picked up the plutonium."

We went up to our room to compose a report to Salinas, and while we were working on it Kim called. "I spoke to my mom, and she said she's been to Kurokawa's house twice," she said. "He often hosts fundraisers for his environmental causes. She said he has a huge arsenal of weapons and he loves to show them off."

"What kind of weapons?"

"Everything from handguns to semi-automatic rifles. I asked her if she was insane to go back a second time, and she said he was sweet—that he cares so much for animals." She snorted. "I told her that if she ever goes back there I'll have her committed."

"Good to know he's heavily armed," I said. "Anything else?"

"I called a couple of guys I know in the Idaho State Police," she said. "They told me he's a nut job but basically harmless. I beg to disagree, but what do I know? I just check for fishing licenses, right? I'm not a real cop."

"You seem pretty real to me," I said. "Thanks for the information." I promised to keep in touch with her, and invited her and Cindy to come out to Honolulu sometime and meet my family, and she said they'd already been talking about a trip next winter.

We finished our email to Salinas and told him we were going out to look for information on Kurokawa. Then Ray said, "You know what he's going to say, don't you?"

"Salinas?"

"He's going to want us to head up to Duncan's place. It's the best lead we have."

"Then let's do it." The excitement of the chase was building. We had a target and a place to go. Even if we were completely wrong, at least we were doing something.

The earliest flight Ray could find would take us to Spokane that evening. Assuming that Salinas agreed, we'd pick up a car and spend the night at a hotel near the airport.

By then the sun had come out, and the snow looked like it had begun to melt. Our rental car had come with a long-handled gizmo with a broom on one end and an ice scraper on the other, and Ray and I traded using it to clear the rental car off. By the time we were done I was frozen through and my gloves were wet. Ray turned the heater on full blast as we pulled out of the parking lot and I leaned forward to warm up.

It was a bumpy ride into town. "Goddamn potholes," Ray said, clenching the steering wheel. "Can't see them with all this snow."

"Better you than me," I said, as the car slid forward on a patch of ice. By then I was trusting Ray's driving skills in snow and ice more completely, so I only clenched the door handle—didn't gasp or press my foot to an imaginary brake pedal.

We drove to the address we had for Kurokawa, a sprawling ranch house on the edge of town, and identified ourselves to the officer in the unmarked car who was watching the premises. He gave us a couple of leads—the closest barber shop, grocery and so on.

We spent the next couple of hours talking to people, showing them Kurokawa's photograph and asking questions. Most people knew of his environmental activities, but no one said they'd seen him in a while. The guy who cut his hair said that Brian hadn't been in for a couple of months, and that he vaguely remembered hearing he was going to stay with some friends in the panhandle for a while.

We were eating lunch in a café a few blocks from Kurokawa's house when Salinas called. "Any new leads since your last message?" he asked.

All we had was the barber's memory.

"All signs seem to indicate he's allied himself with this Duncan guy," Salinas said.

"Let me guess," I said. "You want us to fly up there."

"You guys from HPD are sharp," Salinas said.

"We're already booked on a flight this evening to Spokane," I said. "We won't get in until late tonight, though."

"Good job. Keep me in the loop."

We spent the afternoon pounding the pavement, so to speak, discovering nothing new about Brian Kurokawa. Before it got dark we returned our rental car and settled down at the gate for our flight.

We still didn't have confirmation that Kurokawa was the guy who'd picked up the plutonium, but since we had no other leads we were continuing to chase him. It was going to be a huge downer if we found out he'd just been out bird-watching or something. And it would push our investigation back, giving whoever did have the plutonium an additional head start toward using it.

It had begun to snow lightly again and I was glad to be getting out of Idaho Falls. What a huge change it must have been for my granny, growing up in this cold, snowy place, and then being transported to the endless sunshine of Hawai'i. I said a silent thank you to her first husband, the fervent Mormon who had brought her to Laie, as well as my gratitude to him for dying so she could meet my grandfather and spawn my father and his siblings.

We were on the small twin-engine plane when the pilot announced we would be delayed for a short time. "We're just going to taxi over to the de-icing pad," he said. "Shouldn't take us too long to get cleaned up."

"What does that mean?" I asked Ray. "They want the plane clean before takeoff?"

"It's no big deal," he said. "When the ice and snow build up on the wings and the fuselage it adds extra weight to the plane." He shook his head. "You really need to get out more."

I was nervous the whole flight, worrying about a buildup of ice or snow on the plane, and only could breathe freely when we were back on the ground. We checked our email once more before going to bed, and found a message from Salinas that there was "increased activity" detected around the complex where Art Duncan and his followers lived.

The email ended with, "Check in with the resident agency in Spokane and liaise with them. Then proceed with caution."

21 – Blind Squirrel

After we finished going through our email, I pulled out the map that had come with the rental car.

"You've got to be kidding me," I said, as I found the tiny hamlet of Eagan's Gap on the map.

"About what?"

"This guy Duncan? Guess where he lives."

"In a house?"

"Yeah, in a house. On the edge of something called the Lolo National Forest."

In Hawaiian, the word "lolo" meant crazy. Sure was the right place for a bunch of lunatics to gather. "In good weather it should take us close to two hours." I peered out through the hotel room window at the parking lot, illuminated by a couple of mercury vapor lamps. "And that doesn't look like good weather."

Ray leaned back against the headboard of his bed. "Why don't we try something different this time. Instead of rushing in to a place we don't know anything about, suppose we put together a plan first."

"You know, it's like I always say about you, Ray. Even a blind squirrel finds a nut now and then. I think that's a great idea."

He tossed a box of tissues at me, which I ducked. "Blind squirrel!"

"Hey, it's an expression. And since we don't have squirrels in Hawai'i, I never get to use it."

"Fine. Then you come up with the first idea."

I went through everything we knew about Brian Kurokawa, which wasn't much. "We have a sort of in with Kurokawa. Kim's mother knows him."

"She said her mother donated to him. That's not the same as knowing him."

"Yeah, but she's been to his house. And this is a small community. What if we ask Kim's mother to make an introduction for us?"

"Assuming Kurokawa is out there with Duncan. What does that get us?"

"Hey, I'm working on it."

We sat in silence for a moment or two, the heater beneath the window buzzing, and then Ray said, "Suppose we pretend to be rich guys interested in donating to his cause? That might lure him out of Duncan's compound."

"What's our rationale for being out there in the middle of nowhere, though?"

"Hunting? Fishing?"

"A, it's the middle of winter. B, the guy's a wildlife conservationist. Not going to want to talk to hunters or fishermen."

We both went on line, looking for inspiration. I found a website that indicated the largest specimens of mountain lions had been found in the Idaho panhandle and I started to put together an idea. It took a while but finally I said, "Let's try this on for size. You and I are friends from Honolulu and we travel around taking photos of different species of wildlife."

"Okay."

"The Idaho panhandle is famous for mountain lions. Let's say that we've come out here to do some kind of photographic safari— hired a guide to take us out so we can get some shots of big cats."

"In the winter."

I shrugged. "It's when we can get away. And mountain lions don't hibernate so they're out at dawn and dusk hunting for deer."

"Okay. So we're here to take pictures of mountain lions. And?"

"And I made contact with my cousin in Idaho Falls, and her mom told us about Brian and his preservation efforts. We say that we're in Idaho Falls and can we meet to talk about a donation?"

"But he's not there, and neither are we."

"That's true. So let's assume he writes back and says, sorry, I'm up near Spokane, and then we write back to say no problem, we're heading that way ourselves."

"What if he doesn't write back?"

"I know, the plan has a lot of holes in it. But have you got anything better, Mr. Blind Squirrel?"

"Don't make me come over there," Ray said, but there was laughter behind his voice. "Fine. But we're going to need some background for us so we seem reasonable. What do we do for a living that gets us the kind of money to travel around and make big donations?"

I thought about that for a minute. My dad had spent most of his career as a contractor in Honolulu, building everything from houses to small shopping centers. By the time he retired, he owned a couple of properties that provided a generous income for him and my mother. I could extrapolate that.

"How'd you like to own a couple of shopping centers?" I asked Ray.

"With pleasure."

I explained my idea and Ray agreed. "As long as I don't have to pretend any technical expertise."

Brian Kurokawa would certainly want to check our bona fides before agreeing to meet us, and the easiest way to accomplish that quickly was a solid website. Dakota was taking a web design course at UH, I called his cell. "You back from Japan?" he asked.

"Not exactly. Back in the States, at least. I need your help with a website. You think you could put together something quick for me?"

I explained what I wanted someone to see. "You're going to need a lot of material to make it seem reasonable," Dakota said. "Pictures, text, a list of properties. I can do the tech stuff but I don't know anything about shopping centers."

"I do. If I pull the stuff together and email it to you, you can make it all work?"

"Absolutely."

From memory, I typed up a quick list of the shopping centers my father had built, all of them since sold. I emailed that list to Ray and he began finding photos online of each center, along with whatever statistics he could find—date of construction, gross leasable area, and so on.

Using the template of a website for another small shopping center company and began writing the copy that would pull it all together. It reminded me of drafting term papers back in the day, when I'd stay up late at the clunky IBM PC my parents had bought me, surrounded by source material and notes, trying to make sense out of chaos.

I knew that if I called Mike with an update he'd just complain, so I took the coward's way out and texted him that Ray and I were okay, that we were in Spokane.

It was close to two o'clock in the morning when I sent the last of the material to Dakota, with a plea to get it done as soon as possible.

It was pouring when Ray and I woke up on Thursday morning, but at least the rain washed away most of the snow outside. The room's heater had been working overtime keeping a stable temperature of seventy two degrees—winter in Hawai'i.

Dakota had come through like a star—he had bought a website for us in the name we'd come up, and had set up a home page with information on the company, and a page for each of the shopping centers we were pretending to own.

It was the thinnest of backgrounds—if Brian Kurokawa did any digging at all, he'd discover that the whole thing was a sham. But it was good enough for government work, as they say.

From Kim Carhartt, I got her mother's phone number, then called and introduced myself.

"Yes, Kim told me that she met you," she said. She had a slight accent, much like Mike's mother. "Your mother is Japanese too?"

"Half," I said. "My Ojisan came to Hawai'i from Tokushima Prefecture to work in the cane fields and met my grandmother, who was native Hawaiian." We talked through the genealogy for a couple of minutes.

"I wanted to ask you about Brian Kurokawa," I said, when we'd gotten all that out of the way. "Kim said you've been to his house a couple of times?"

"Yes, he is a very earnest man. So dedicated to his cause."

"Would he know who you are if you contacted him?"

"Oh, yes. We have had many conversations about Japanese people in Idaho."

I asked her if she could put us in touch with him. "I do not have his phone number but I have exchanged emails with him. I could try to send him a message. Is this police work?"

"I don't want him to know that Ray and I work for the FBI." I explained the cover story that we had created, and gave her our fake names, the company name and the website address.

"I am sure he will want to talk to you," she said. "He is always looking for money."

She agreed to write him an email, but send it to me to check over before she actually contacted him, to make sure she got everything right.

While I was speaking to her, Ray had called the resident agency in Spokane and spoken to an agent there, who suggested we come in for a meeting and to get up to speed on what they knew about Duncan.

We decided to have a good breakfast at the hotel because we had no idea what would be facing us out in Eagan's Gap. We loaded up on eggs, home fries, bacon and juice and sat at a table that looked out on the icy parking lot and the looming gray clouds.

Before we left the motel, we checked our email once again, and

I saw the message that Kim's mother had drafted. I made a couple of minor adjustments and sent it back to her, along with an email address I used that had no connection to my real name or my law enforcement work. I asked her to give that address to Kurokawa.

She responded almost immediately that she'd contact him and see what he said. Then Ray drove our rented sedan into downtown Spokane, where the resident agency was located in a glassy high-rise building. We parked in the adjacent garage and walked through a sky bridge.

Marla Cohen was a motherly-looking woman in her mid-fifties, and she led us back to an office with a big picture window looking out toward snow-capped mountains. "Honolulu, huh," she said, as we sat down. "How'd you luck into an assignment there?"

"We're actually homicide cops," I said. "On loan to the JTTF."

She nodded. "Which explains your interest in Art Duncan. We've got at least a gigabyte of digital information on him, but I'll give you the high points. Very smart guy, PhD in physics from MIT, went to work at the Lawrence Livermore Labs on nuclear weapon development right after he graduated. Spent about ten years there, growing increasingly frustrated because he wanted to be able to deploy the bombs he was designing against America's enemies."

She laced her fingers together and leaned back in her chair a bit. "He and his wife Bethany picked up and moved to Idaho about eight years ago. They bought a hundred acres of land and invited some like-minded folks to join them. We believe there are about fifty people out there now. They're as self-sufficient as they can be— solar and wind power, their own school for the kids. Duncan himself teaches the science classes."

"Sounds utopian," I said.

"And it is, except for their ideology, which is to bomb everybody who doesn't agree with them back to the Stone Age."

"U.S. targets?" Ray asked.

"Just the opposite. They're all very gung-ho patriots and believe we need to take a stronger stand against our enemies. They advocate bombing places like Afghanistan and Iraq. They're willing to accept a lot of collateral damage if they can wipe out non-state actors like ISIS and Al-Qaeda."

"Have they carried out any actions?" I asked.

"Not as far as we know. We have an undercover operative placed within the organization, and he feeds us regular updates. Duncan has been perfecting a small nuclear weapon that can be deployed by an unmanned drone. Supposedly he's been waiting for the final ingredient."

"Plutonium," Ray said. "We think he might have that by now."

We explained the background of our case, from the crash of the Usagi Maru to our discovery that the plutonium stolen from the Fukushima Dai-Ichi plant had been divided into two shipments.

"We have reason to believe that Brian Kurokawa picked up the plutonium in Seattle on Sunday and is either on his way to Eagan's Gap or already there."

"That's scary. I don't have a way to get in touch with my agent. I have to wait for him to reach out to me. But if what you say is correct he should be in touch soon."

"We're trying to arrange a meeting with Kurokawa." I explained about our connection, through Kim's mother. "That could confirm whether he's with Duncan or not."

Agent Cohen offered to print out a basic dossier for us, and while she did that I checked the email account that I'd given to Kim's mother. Nothing there but junk.

We spent the morning at the office, reading through everything Cohen had been able to print out for us, and doing our own research on wildlife photography, mountain lions, and Brian Kurokawa's many demonstrations and arrests.

It was early afternoon when an email from him came through. As I'd hoped, he said that he'd be happy to meet with us, but he wasn't in Idaho Falls. "But if you get up to Coeur d'Alene, let me know."

Bingo. I wrote back right away that we had been thinking of heading that way, that we wanted to try an outlook at a place called

Petty Creek, where we could photograph bighorn sheep, golden eagles, and if we were lucky a mountain lion. Was he anywhere near there?

While I waited for a response, I found an article he'd written for a right-wing online journal. In it, he wrote about the way wildlife has rebounded after the Chernobyl incident.

> *Yes, the animals can have high levels of radioactivity, as the radioactive matter in the ground moves up through the food chain, but they're surviving. The Eurasian lynx has been extinct in Europe for more than a hundred years with almost the entire population living in Siberia, but now they've rebounded. The same story is true for the moose and the white-tailed eagle.*

He listed a lot of statistics and the more I read, the more plausible the idea became. I could see him believing he could convert vast swaths of Afghanistan and Iraq into wildlife preserves if he could just wipe out those pesky humans in the area.

Kurokawa emailed back a while later. If we got off I-90 at Petty Creek, we could take the frontage road up to the small town of Alberton, and he could meet us at a café there. He suggested early afternoon the next day, Friday.

I wrote back right away and made plans to meet him at the café at one o'clock.

That gave us nearly twenty-four hours to put together our plans. I hoped it would be enough time.

22 – A Huge Difference

Ray and I spent the rest of the afternoon beginning to put our plan in motion. "My husband has a couple of cameras you guys can borrow," Agent Cohen said. "Just be careful with them."

"He's a photographer?" I asked.

"He's retired. He followed me all over the country as the Bureau moved me, so when it was time for him to stop working I agreed to take this post. He's a big outdoors guy and it killed him when we lived in Chicago and Boston."

"Tell us about the agent you have inside the compound," Ray said.

"He was part of the ROTC program in college, and served two tours in Iraq. After he returned to the States, he went through training at Quantico where he was identified as a candidate for this operation. The Bureau created an identity for him based on his real background and he began building the credentials that could get him admitted to Duncan's inner circle—social media posts, online contact and so on."

She sat back in her chair. "He moved into the compound about six months ago, first working on a security detail. Now he teaches the older teens military strategies. He's using the name Augie Lenox."

We went back to the small conference room and read the information that Lenox had assembled, beginning with background on the fifty or so people living at the compound. One cluster was well-educated but like Duncan, disgusted with the way our government had pandered to terrorists. They included a number of teachers, a doctor and a pair of nurses who kept the group healthy, and a Baptist minister and his wife who held services in their home and ran a small Sunday school. A couple of men with engineering backgrounds maintained the computer network and the solar panels that powered everything.

Another thirty men and women, all American-born whites, worked in manual labor, farming or maintaining the compound. According to Lenox, many of them felt marginalized by immigrants willing to take low-wage jobs and the prevalence of Spanish in most big cities. The only foreign languages taught in the compound's schools were Arabic and Farsi, so that the next generation of soldiers could understand their enemies.

Duncan had also recruited a sizable number of military veterans, male and female, who had seen American's enemies up close and wanted to continue the fight. Some of them had translation skills, while others patrolled the compound or worked with Duncan on long-range tactical plans.

What concerned me most was the presence of children at the compound. The minister and his wife had four children, and there were another fifteen kids, ranging in age from infants to teenagers. It seemed deeply irresponsible to me to raise kids in such an environment, and I worried that some of them might be killed or injured if the Bureau carried out a raid on the compound.

By the time we left the office it was six o'clock and we were both overwhelmed with the data the Bureau had collected. It was a dark, moonless night, and the streets were empty, the stores closed, and the only lighting came from mercury vapor lamps.

"It's creepy, but I'm beginning to understand Duncan's mindset," I said, as Ray drove. "You can't blame the guy for trying to protect the United States."

"Just the way he's going about doing it," Ray said.

"You think if our government was more proactive, they'd be able to make more progress against terrorists?"

"You mean dropping bombs?"

"It worked to shut down World War II." I held up my hand. "Not that I'm advocating the kind of wholesale bombing Duncan wants to do. But don't you feel frustrated sometimes? We're doing what we can to make the world a safer place for our kids, but what we do is such small beans compared to the things that terrorists do. One guy puts a bomb in his shoe, and now everybody who flies has to take shoes off. Another jerk plots to use liquid explosives to bring down a plane, and now you can't carry a regular size tube of toothpaste on board."

"And you think bombing them into oblivion would stop that?"

"It's just so frustrating," I said. "When you think about all those evil creeps out there plotting against us, and then you consider, well, if we wiped them out in one fell swoop we'd make the world safer."

"But you'd wipe out a lot of innocent people, too."

"How many of them are really innocent? Suppose you live in some village in Iraq and you know there's an ISIS supporter next door. Aren't you just supporting terrorism by not reporting him?" I sighed. "It's such a slippery slope."

"All we can do is what we can do," Ray said, as he swung into the parking lot for a group of big-box stores on the outskirts of town. "Our little part. And hope that it helps."

We had put together a shopping list of items we needed to make our story more legitimate. I couldn't keep wearing Mike's oversized coat, for example, because it looked like I'd bought it at a thrift store. Not something a rich guy would do.

We shopped for outdoor gear at the sporting goods store, including microfiber shirts and good-quality hiking boots. At the register, I verified that we could return what we didn't use. "Just keep the receipts," the clerk said.

We ate dinner at a brewpub near the airport, and between courses we went over our plans, stopping to think through as many details as we could. By the time we returned to the motel I was exhausted but also excited about what the next day would hold. I hoped we'd get enough information from Brian Kurokawa to trigger a raid on Duncan's compound, and take the whole group down, as well as retrieving the stolen plutonium.

"I want to talk to Julie," Ray said. "I'm heading down to the lobby."

"That's cool. I'll call Mike."

I sat back on the bed and dialed Mike's number. "Hey," I said, when he answered.

"Who's this? The display on my phone reads Kimo. I used to know a guy by that name but I haven't seen him in ages."

"Very funny. How are you?"

"Bored. Horny. Maybe I'll head out to a club later. See if I can meet a guy who's interested in having sex with me."

"I'm interested, believe me."

"Yeah, but you're not here."

"I could be, if you close your eyes."

"Phone sex? Give me a break."

"Well, what do you want from me? I'd much rather be home with you than stuck here where it's freezing cold. Ray's great, but he's not so good at cuddling up as you are."

Mike snorted. "How's your case going?"

"Closing in," I said. "We met with a guy today who gave us some information, and it looks like we might be ready to make a move soon."

"Be careful, K. I want you home in one piece."

"Not to worry. Ray and I are just small cogs in a big machine. We'll be well behind the SWAT guys, I guarantee you."

"Tell Ray I'll kick his ass if anything happens to you."

I told him I would, that I loved him and missed him and would see him soon.

The next morning Ray and I were both too keyed up to eat much, and we landed at the resident agency in Spokane early. Agent Cohen was already there.

"I got a message last night from Augie Lenox," she said. "Kurokawa arrived at the compound two days ago. Lenox saw him carrying in a box but couldn't see what was in it."

"The plutonium," I said.

She nodded. "Duncan is currently locked up in his lab with a couple of assistants. Lenox feels there's a big action in the wind, and that Duncan has found a way to transport a weapon to the Middle East and deploy it in territory controlled by ISIS or Al-Qaida."

We left soon after, because the roads were icy and we wanted to be sure to make it to our rendezvous with Kurokawa before one o'clock. Ray drove because we decided we'd rather not end up sliding into a ditch.

On the way, I went back to the conversation we'd had the day before. "I wonder what'll happen if we shut down Duncan's operation. Will somebody else just spring up to fill the void? Is there already somebody out there who's planning the same thing?"

"Even if there is, we still have to shut Duncan down. We're talking nuclear weapons, Kimo. You can't just target a terrorist cell. Duncan wants to wipe out entire civilizations."

"And isn't it that civilization's responsibility to control violence among its members? The places Duncan wants to bomb are failed states that aren't capable of policing their radical elements. By wiping out the terrorists there, he's protecting the rest of the world."

"I hope you're just being the devil's advocate," Ray said, gripping the steering wheel as he navigated us over an icy patch. "Because none of us are qualified to play God and decide who lives or dies."

"I agree. And I'm not saying I'm going to jump ship and join Duncan. Just that he has a point. If he has the skill and the material to protect American lives, doesn't he have the responsibility to use them? Yes, innocent people in Iraq or Somalia or wherever will die. But they're just as likely to be killed by their neighbors. And if it comes down to killing a bunch of Iraqis or Pakistanis to protect Addie and Owen and Mike and the rest of my family, I'm all in."

"This is why it's tough to work in law enforcement," Ray said. "Because we have to look at both sides of the issue, and then follow the law and our own consciences."

"What if they come in conflict?"

"That's what prayer is for, my friend."

We were quiet for the rest of the trip. Gray stone peaks, covered with snow and dotted with evergreens, loomed on both sides of the highway, hemming us in. We were trapped as much as our country was, surrounded by intractable enemies, and the sheer size of the mountains around us was intimidating.

We had some time before our scheduled meeting with Kurokawa, so we drove down along the winding country road to the bighorn viewing area at Petty Creek. The creek itself ran beside us, choked with boulders and ice, and we startled a big buck drinking from it as we passed. He took off, loping up into higher ground.

Ray pulled up and parked facing a snow-covered meadow. The mountains around us were shrouded in white, leafless trees and the occasional pine interspersed between patches of white on the ground.

I felt totally isolated from the rest of the world, and I could see why Duncan had chosen the area for his compound, even though I was freezing my cojones off.

As we sat there in the car with the heat blasting, I saw some movement at the edge of the woods. "Look over there," I said.

A bighorn sheep, gray-white with those distinctive horns, raced out of the woods into a flat, snow-covered field, followed by another of similar size. "Get the cameras out," I said and I quickly fumbled for the one Agent Cohen had lent to me. I rolled down the window and started snapping shots as quickly as I could, as the sheep charged each other and butted horns.

I switched to movie mode and filmed their challenge for a couple of minutes. Then, as quickly as they'd arrived, they were gone. I raised the window up and looked at the footage I'd taken. "This is so cool," I said, even though my fingers were so frozen it was hard to operate the controls. "Look what I've got."

I had a great two minutes of the sheep fighting each other, and Ray had taken a bunch of good shots he could edit down to close-ups. "We'll have to show these to Kurokawa," I said. "It'll help cement our cover story."

As he backed out of the parking space, I thought about the scene we'd just witnessed. There was something very primal about it—in the same way that we were planning our own attack on Kurokawa. We'd have to be a lot more subtle than butting heads, though, if we expected to get anything useful out of him.

We drove back up to Alberton, the small town where Kurokawa had suggested we meet at a café called Big I. We parked the rental car in front and hurried through the cold, eager to get inside and warm up. "I miss Hawai'i," I said, as I pulled the door open.

The café was charming, with mismatched tables and chairs and lots of posters and photographs of scenic Idaho on the walls. It was nice and toasty and I was eager to shuck my brand new parka. An elderly couple sat at one table by the plate-glass window that looked out on the street. The beauty outside was a stark contrast to the evil that we believed was lurking out there in the woods.

A cheerful woman in a flowered apron came out from behind the counter. "Two?"

"We'll be three," I said. I asked for a table toward the back, and Ray and I chose the two seats that faced out.

"The trout's fresh-caught this morning," she said, as she handed us a paper menu. "The bison's grass-fed and the new potatoes come from a hothouse farm a few miles away."

I hadn't expected to find a farm-to-table restaurant in the backwoods of Idaho, but I was happy we'd stumbled onto it. We were perusing the menu when the front door opened, bringing in a gust of cold air.

Brian Kurokawa was dressed like a wilderness guide—floppy canvas hat, down jacket bristling with pockets, cargo pants and heavy boots. I waved him over and we introduced ourselves.

"I'm always glad to meet fellow wildlife advocates," he said, as he sat with us. "Have you ordered? I've been told the trout is terrific here, but I don't eat anything with eyes."

We chatted for a couple of minutes about our visit, both of us trying to stay as close to the truth as possible. "My mom's been doing some genealogy research and she discovered a branch of the family still in my grandmother's home town, Idaho Falls," I said. "When I got in touch with my cousin there, she invited us to come visit and take some pictures. This was the only time we could both get away."

"I checked out your company's website," he said. "I really like your dad's philosophy, that he wouldn't build something in a natural area, because he didn't want to disturb the native wildlife."

I was particularly pleased with that note—which though untrue did sound like something my father might have said.

"I want to put up a site of my own someday, with some of the photos Ray and I have been taking," I said. "Hey, I have to show you this video we took this morning."

I pulled out the camera and showed him the video of the bighorn sheep, and Ray showed him some of the stills he'd taken. "You're lucky you got something so good so quickly," Brian said. "I have a blind set up on the edge of my friend's property, overlooking a stream where white-tailed deer come to drink, and sometimes when it gets too hectic I retreat up there. Nobody else knows that it exists and I can hide out as long as I want."

The waitress brought our food, and as we ate, I asked Brian how he'd got involved in wildlife activism.

"I was in veterinary school at Washington State when I joined a protest against logging at Saint Joe National Forest—not too far south of here. It opened my eyes to the way that we've been systematically decimating the natural environment. When I got back to school I had a crisis of conscience. Did I want to make a career out of taking care of pampered pets? Or did I want to try and make a real difference in the lives of animals? You can see which path I chose."

"I think it's admirable," I said. "I'm part native Hawaiian, and our culture has always had a special connection to the land, the ocean, and the creatures who share the planet with us. We even have this tradition of the ʻaumakua, a spirit animal who protects us."

"I've heard of those. Do you have one?"

I nodded. "They tend to run in families—they also represent our ancestors. My family's ʻaumakua is the dolphin."

"How cool. I have a similar relationship with the *kitsune*—it's a small Japanese fox. I used to dream about one when I was a little kid, and a couple of times I've seen red foxes in woods here. The first time was right before the police arrived to arrest me when I was trespassing on a logging trail. Ever since, whenever I see a fox I consider it a warning of trouble."

He finished his wild mushroom omelet and said, "So, how do you think you can help the cause?"

"Why don't you tell us what you need," Ray said. "I thought your base of operations was down in Idaho Falls. Have you moved up here?"

"Just for the short term," he said. "I've been working with a guy who has some big plans. I can't say too much right now, but what we're hoping to create is a couple of huge wildlife preserves in the Middle East, where all kinds of local endangered species can repopulate and thrive."

"Interesting. Right in the middle of a war zone?" I asked.

"If our plans come through, there won't be anyone in the area left to wage war," he said. "And certainly, a lot of animals will die at first as we wipe the slate clean, but eventually they'll rebound, just like they've done after Chernobyl."

I remembered the online article he'd written, and I saw what had motivated him to join forces with Art Duncan.

"What I can use right now is money to charter a private jet," he said. "I need one that's capable of flying across the Pacific, and that's going to cost at least twenty grand each way. Can you help out with that?"

"How soon would you need the money?"

"As soon as possible. We have a tentative flight scheduled for this weekend, if all goes well and I can raise the cash."

I looked at Ray. "What do you think?"

"We can manage forty grand between us, can't we?"

I nodded. "I'd have to move some money around and that might take a day or two," I said. "I assume you can handle a wire transfer?"

"Of course."

"How can we get in touch with you once we're ready?" I asked.

"You can use the same email address. I'll send you the routing information."

We chatted for a few more minutes, and then Brian had to go. "Thanks for your support," he said. "You're going to make a huge difference in wildlife conservation."

"That's just what we want to do," I said as we shook hands.

23 – Isolation

Brian Kurokawa left us with the check, which didn't surprise me. We paid and drove back to Spokane through more ice and rain.

"He seems like such a good guy," I said. "Too bad he got roped into Duncan's craziness."

"He's not so good," Ray said. "You saw his record. He's as much of a terrorist as any of them, even if you like the ideas behind what he's doing."

By the time we got back to the resident agency, it was late in the afternoon, and the sun was setting over the foothills of the Rocky Mountains. We parked in the same garage and crossed the glass connector once more. This time, though, I noticed the network of covered skywalks around us, lit up against the darkness, and I marveled at the desire to live in a place where you had to isolate yourself so much from the natural world.

My cell rang with an "unknown" number. "FBI, Detective Kanapa'aka."

"Detective? It's Dylan Hart from Port Townsend. We found Endo's brother."

"You did? That's great. Where is he? Can we talk to him?"

"You can talk to him, but he won't answer," Hart said. "He's dead."

I turned the speaker on my phone so Ray could hear. "Eiji Endo is dead? What happened?"

"This morning a trooper was doing a routine check at the Indian

John Hill rest stop along eastbound I-90," he said. "A couple of miles east of Cle Elum. Little over an hour east of Seattle. The trooper noticed some disturbed landscaping in the woods off the parking area and discovered the body of an Asian male approximately thirty years of age. I saw the alert come through and emailed over the photo you gave me. Just heard back from the Kittitas County Coroner in Ellensburg with a tentative ID."

"Cause of death?" Ray asked.

"Two bullets to the rear of the brain, fired at close range," Hart said.

We thanked him, and asked him to put whoever was investigating the murder in touch with us. When I ended the call, I turned to Ray. "My cousin Kim's mother said that Brian Kurokawa has a lot of weapons at his house." "But why would he kill Endo's brother?" Ray asked. "The guy probably didn't even speak much English, and Endo said that Kurokawa doesn't speak much Japanese, if any. Why not just dump him out of the car and leave him there?"

"Because he could identify Kurokawa, and connect him to the plutonium," I said.

"Then why not kill Hiroto Endo, too?"

I shrugged. "Maybe because he knew Hiroto was heading back to Japan right away?"

Eiji Endo's death reminded us that we were dealing with people who were willing to wipe out innocent civilians at any moment.

We set up our laptops in the conference room once more and checked for new emails at both our Bureau and personal addresses. Mike had sent me a cartoon of a polar bear on a surfboard with a note that he missed me.

Then I checked the email account I'd been using to correspond with Brian Kurokawa. Only a couple of new spam messages since the last time I'd cleaned up, and right in the middle, an email from Brian.

"Thanks for your support—your donation will help make the earth a better place for all creatures," he wrote, in what was probably a packaged message. Beneath it was the routing information to use when sending the payment to him.

"Look at this," I said, showing the message to Ray.

"Pretty cool customer," Ray said. "If he killed Eiji Endo he certainly didn't seem upset when we met with him. And now here he is, asking for his money."

"He's a sociopath, what do you expect?"

"Actually he's probably more like a psychopath," Ray said. "If you want to get technical about it. Psychopaths are more likely to be manipulative and charming, without empathy for other people. Kurokawa's educated and organized, whereas a sociopath would be more emotional, disorganized and volatile."

"Thank you for that clinical definition," I said. "Good to have a trained sociologist on the team."

"You're welcome, Mr. English Major," Ray said. "When I need grammar advice I'll be sure to come to you."

He looked at me and I looked back at him, and then we both began to laugh.

I went back to the bank information Kurokawa had sent. It began with an eight-digit code which I figured out, through a bit of online research, was the SWIFT code, a standard bank identifier used for intra-bank transfers, particularly international ones. The first four characters were letters, for the bank code. I looked them up and discovered they had been assigned to Banco Mantarraya S.A. I found a website that indicated it was a private bank headquartered in Grand Cayman.

The next two characters were the country code, in this case KY. The two that followed were the location code, in this case the same KY. Then the ten-digit account number where the money was to be deposited.

I sat there staring at the letters and numbers on the screen. There was something else I ought to look at. Some other clue, some other connection.

There had been two wire transfers—to Akiro Suzuki and Raiden

Kameda, and Jutta Dore had told us that both came from the same Cayman Islands account. I looked through all my notes but I couldn't find any record of the actual account number.

Ray didn't have it either.

I checked the world time clock converter. It was Saturday morning in Tokyo, so I called Jutta Dore's cell phone. "I might be on to something," I said, after we'd said hello. "Can you find me the Cayman Islands routing information for the payments to Suzuki and Kameda?"

"It'll take a little digging. I'll email it to you in a couple of minutes."

We hung up, and I drilled my fingers against the tabletop. "Can you stop that, please?" Ray asked. "You're making me crazy."

"This could be the link we need," I said. "If the wire transfer information matches, we'll have a clear connection between Brian Kurokawa and the theft of the plutonium."

"I understand. But we already know that, don't we? We know that Kurokawa picked up the box from Hiroto Endo's ship."

"We know that Endo picked up a box from Kameda. We know he delivered that box to Kurokawa. But we have no concrete proof of what's in the box, do we? That means we still don't have enough to convince a judge to issue a search warrant for Duncan's compound."

"How do you prove to the judge that there's actually plutonium in the box?" Ray asked. "Suppose Kameda gave all the plutonium to the Griffins and sent Endo with a dummy box."

"Why would he do that? The whole purpose of splitting the plutonium into two parts was to double the chance that some of it would reach the States."

We went back and forth for a while over what we had, what we didn't have, and what we needed, and finally my email pinged with an incoming message from Jutta Dore.

I opened a second window with the message from Kurokawa, and checked the numbers three times before I said, "The numbers don't match."

"What?" Ray asked.

I shifted my laptop so he could see. "Both accounts are in the Cayman Islands—see the KY there? But they're at different banks."

"Call Dore again," Ray said.

"What's the point? It's a dead end."

"Not necessarily," he said. "Didn't Dore say that the Japanese police were able to subpoena bank records for Watanabe's account? If Kurokawa bought the plutonium from him, there'll be a transfer from his account to Watanabe's."

I called Dore again. "We need as much information as you have on Watanabe's account." I explained about looking for a transfer between the two accounts.

"I'm not sure we'll have that, but I'll check."

It was killing me to have to wait a second time, but this time the message came through more quickly. Unfortunately it was a PDF, a mess of numbers and Japanese text, interspersed with a bunch of SWIFT codes. I couldn't figure out what it all meant.

I scrolled through it, my hopes sinking, until I realized that I could search the file for Kurokawa's account number. My fingers were twitching as I copied the account number from Brian's email and pasted it into the search box on the PDF.

It took me a moment to understand what I was reading. Then I crowed to Ray, "The numbers match!"

He came to look at my screen again, and we both checked the numbers several times. Back in December, Kurokawa had made a transfer of a half-million yen to Watanabe's account. And then, the day before, he'd sent another half-million, in addition to whatever he'd paid Endo in dollars.

After that, everything shifted into high gear. It was still afternoon in Honolulu, so we got Francisco Salinas and Marla Cohen on a conference call, along with a couple of agents from the Seattle office who had been working on Duncan's case.

I explained the way we'd matched the bank routing information and account number. "We can connect Kurokawa, and by extension Duncan, to the money paid for the plutonium," I said. "As well as to the shooting death of a Japanese national, one of the two men who brought the plutonium to the U.S. from Japan."

I walked them through our train of thought, from the purchase of the plutonium from Akiro Suzuki to its sale to an account controlled by Jiro Watanabe. Then Kurokawa's two transfers to Watanabe. Endo's identification of Kurokawa, and then his brother's murder at the rest stop outside Cle Elum.

"My operative inside the compound confirms that Kurokawa arrived with something the other day, and that Duncan and his assistants are locked up in their lab," Agent Cohen said. "I need to remind you that this property is very isolated and we only have limited intel about what's going on there."

"Kurokawa told us that has a private jet booked for this weekend," Ray added. "So there's a real time pressure here."

"He's not getting the money for the jet from us, though," I said. "Although we can't eliminate the possibility that he has other sponsors out there, or that he's able to swing the charter on credit."

We walked away from the meeting with our assignments. A SWAT team would fly in from the Seattle office. The SAC in Seattle would arrange the Federal warrants necessary for our raid. Other agents would review the layout of the compound from drawings provided by Augie Lenox. Agent Cohen would liaise with the Shoshone County Sheriff's department.

Ray and I worked on a big research project—tracking the names of those resident at the compound against weapons permits. Not the most glamorous of jobs but it would be useful to know how much firepower we might be up against.

We stayed at the resident agency until well after dark, then ate dinner at restaurant near our motel. After dinner, I called Mike but I couldn't reach him. I checked the time and thought maybe he was still investigating a case—sometimes he shut his phone off if he was at a fire so that he could focus. I was pretty certain that he hadn't followed through on his threat to go out to a gay club in search of a sex partner. I couldn't even think about that, though.

I left him a message, that it looked like things were going to wrap up in a couple of days, and then I'd be home. "Love you, miss you, sweetheart," I said.

That night I had weird dreams about arriving at the compound to discover that Mike had moved in there with Addie and Owen. They'd sailed up the Snake River in a powerboat driven by the ghost of Eiji Endo. When I confronted Mike he told me that my mother had sent him there with the twins as part of her genealogy research.

I woke up sweaty and disoriented, and the first thing I did was check my phone for messages from Mike, and then my email. Still nothing, and I worried. Was he all right? Was he mad at me for not keeping in touch more? We'd had that conversation a couple of times, when I was swamped with an investigation and I hadn't kept calling to reassure him that I was all right. Maybe he was giving me a dose of my own medicine.

Either way, I was eager to get back to Honolulu. We'd been gone nearly two weeks, between Japan, Washington and Idaho, and I was cold, tired and missing Mike and my family.

24 – Ambush Tactics

Ray and I spent Saturday morning deep in our research projects. I wanted us to be prepared to locate every child at the compound and make sure he or she was safe, so I listed each kid by name, age, and place of residence. Fortunately, the compound had a big social media presence, and I was able to find photos of almost every kid online.

That afternoon, Ray and I joined Agent Cohen and about a dozen others in the conference room at the resident agency's office. "I was able to get in touch with Augie Lenox," Agent Cohen began. "He indicated there's going to be a big party tonight. Based on what he's seen in the past, he expects that tomorrow morning, those who don't sleep in will be at church services at the minister's house. There should be minimal perimeter security and with luck we'll take them by surprise."

"Like George Washington and the Hessians at Trenton," Ray said.

I looked at him. "Mr. American History."

"Hey, I grew up in Pennsylvania. We're big on the Revolutionary War."

"So is Duncan, apparently," Agent Cohen said. "He often uses epithets from the era to refer to himself and his team. Francis Marion was a particular inspiration."

"The Swamp Fox," Ray said. "The father of modern guerilla warfare."

I was impressed and made myself a note to ask Ray more about

Duncan's hero.

The SWAT team leader, a forty-something guy with military bearing, stepped up and introduced himself as Special Agent Geoffrey Sweet. "Here's the operation plan. The Shoshone County Sheriff has identified this high school as a staging area we can use close to Duncan's compound." He brought up a map on his laptop, which played on a screen at one end of the conference room. He used a laser pointer to show us the area east of where Duncan had built his compound.

"We'll rendezvous with the Sheriff's department there at oh-five-hundred," Sweet continued. "Bureau vehicles will leave here at oh-four-fifteen. All agents should come armed and prepared with outdoor gear and bulletproof vests." He looked at Ray and me. "Let me know what you need and we'll provide it."

"What about the kids on the property?" I asked. "What are we doing to protect them?" I showed Sweet my list of kids. "According to Augie Lenox, there's a family dormitory where parents and kids can live. We need to make sure that building is secured quickly to prevent children from getting caught in the crossfire."

"Our first priority is neutralizing perimeter security," Sweet said. "You want to head for the family dorm as soon as you get on property, you do that."

The meeting broke up a few minutes later, and Ray and I met with Sweet. "You have your service weapons?" he asked us.

Both Ray and I shook our head. "We came here via Japan, so we weren't able to take them with us."

"Our quartermaster is driving in with as much firepower as we've got in the office. He'll get you outfitted."

We knew from our work in Kapolei that the quartermaster handled weapons training, storage and distribution. He arrived about an hour later, and issued us both bulletproof vests, rifles on shoulder straps and Glock pistols with extra ammunition cartridges.

"Tell me more about this Swamp Fox guy," I said to Ray, as we drove back to the motel after a long day at the resident agency.

"Pioneer of guerilla warfare," Ray said. "He served in the French and Indian War, and he noticed the way the Cherokee took advantage of cover to hide themselves instead of lining up in their bright red coats. When he began to fight the British, he used the terrain of South Carolina to his advantage and focused on ambush tactics."

"You think Duncan and his group are trying the same things?"

"Hard to say. Based on all the operations he's run, Kurokawa certainly has the knowledge of the landscape, and they would certainly have the home court advantage if they want to fight back against us. But developing nuclear weapons is a more modern approach to warfare than anything Francis Marion ever came up with."

When we got back to the hotel, I called Mike. When he didn't answer again, I got worried and called Dominic. "I was just going to call you," he said. "Mike wasn't sure what country or time zone you were in. Where are you?"

"Spokane, Washington," I said. "But Mike knows that. I've been texting him and talking to him."

"Mike's been out of it for a while," Dominic said.

"What's going on?" I asked, and I could hear the tremor in my voice.

"Soon-O and I woke up around two o'clock this morning to hear Roby barking like mad in the back yard," he said. Back before Mike bought the other half of the duplex, there had been a fence separating the two yards, but he'd torn it down soon after moving in, and we shared one big yard with his parents.

"We turned on the lights and saw Michael splayed out on the yard, Roby standing over him. Haven't gone down those stairs and out into the yard so fast since we first moved in."

"What happened?"

"Hard to say exactly, because Michael's been asleep most of the time since then. But it appears he was watching TV and something went wrong with the satellite, and my brilliant son decided to climb up on the roof and check the dish." He paused. "When we found him, he was knocked out and smelled like a brewery. My guess is that he either fell off the ladder or off the roof."

"Did he break anything?"

"Doesn't look like it. Of course Soon-O and I gave him a thorough going over but it just looks like a concussion. As you know, my son has a very hard head."

"I know. What can I do?" I asked. "I'm stuck here for at least another twenty-four hours. Is there anybody I should call?"

"Don't worry. Dakota's been here most of the day, and your mother is coming by later. Sandra and Cathy are going to bring the twins over tomorrow as soon as Mike feels better."

It was a relief to know that my ohana had pitched in to look after Mike while I wasn't there, but I was still worried about him. "Can you have him call me as soon as he can talk?" I asked.

"Will do. He'll be all right, Kimo."

"I know you'll take care of him." That was the great thing about having a doctor and a nurse as in-laws—anytime we needed medical help or advice, they were there. But I was still freaked out that I couldn't be by Mike's side.

Ray came out of the bathroom and I explained what had happened. "I'm worried he was drinking," I said. "And that I wasn't there to keep him out of trouble."

"His father said he'd be all right," Ray said. "And Dominic's a doctor. He knows."

Ray and Julie attended the same Catholic church as Dom and Soon-O, and they'd become friends as well. "I know," I said. "But I'm still freaking out. I want to be there."

"You can't be," Ray said. "You have a responsibility here. You'll have to be content knowing Mike's in good hands. Think how lucky you are—if something happened to Julie, we don't have family in town like you do. And I know what you're going to say, that your family would jump in. They have in the past, and I appreciate it. But it's not the same."

We went out to a pizzeria nearby for a quick dinner, and I kept looking at my phone to make sure I wasn't missing Mike's call.

"This probably isn't the best time to mention it, " Ray said, as we waited for our pizza. "But Julie and I have been talking about moving back to Philly, so Vinnie can grow up around family. We're just too far away."

"Would you go back to the police department there?"

"Maybe. Maybe a department in the suburbs. Salinas says he might be able to engineer a transfer to the JTTF there. I'm waiting to see."

"You've already been talking to him? Without saying anything to me?"

"It's all just in the exploratory stage," Ray said. "And you said yourself you've been thinking of going back to HPD. The world moves on, Kimo. We have to keep up with it."

25 – Blind

I didn't sleep much Saturday night and I was glad that they had thermoses of coffee for us when we showed up at the resident agency in the morning darkness. There was a palpable tension in the SUV we rode in, a dark cold that came as much from the inside as the outside.

We drove in a caravan of vehicles from Spokane to the rendezvous point, a couple of miles from Duncan's compound. One of the sheriff's deputies opened the high school gym and turned on the high lights. We assembled on the wooden floor and went through our assignments.

"We will approach the property at first light," Agent Sweet said. "SWAT will go in first. They'll be responsible for neutralizing the perimeter security. Once it's clear, the rest of us will move in."

The Hazmat team was responsible for securing the laboratory area, while other teams were assigned to the other buildings. We had a list of all those who Augie Lenox had identified as being in residence, from small children to the elderly. There were six single-family homes, including the one where the minister and his wife lived, and a pair of dormitories for unmarried men and women. Teams were assigned to each building.

"We have two specific targets," Sweet continued. "Art Duncan and Brian Kurokawa. Both of them should be taken alive if at all possible. I'll be heading the team that goes to Duncan's house. Detectives Donne and Kanapa'aka will be with the team for the men's dormitory where we believe Kurokawa is staying, because they've already engaged with him." He looked at me. "Once we've got Kurokawa in custody, then you can look after the children, if that's what you want."

"It doesn't have to be me," I said. "But somebody needs to make sure those kids are safe."

"I'll handle that," one of the agents from Seattle said.

Sweet thanked him. "We all need to remember that these are American citizens who we must assume are enjoying their rights of free assembly and so on. Innocent until proven guilty of anything. So be careful and minimize injury and loss of life."

The SWAT team was to be dropped a mile from the compound so that on-site security would be unprepared for the assault. The rest of us were to wait at that spot for the okay to proceed.

The tension inside our SUV was high as we waited for radio report that all was clear. I couldn't help remembering what Sweet had said about minimizing loss of life and injury, and I hoped the people inside the compound felt the same way.

Finally the radio crackled, and we drove up to the front gate of the compound, which the SWAT team had left open. We poured out with high intensity flashlights and maps of the compound, and Ray and I joined Special Agent Cohen and a pair of agents from Seattle to approach the dormitory.

She went in first, flipping the lights and announcing her presence. There were a half-dozen cots along one wall, three of them occupied, and the men in them were rousted out.

The two agents from Seattle led two of the men away to the main hall, where we were staging everyone. "This is Augie Lenox," Agent Cohen said to us, when they were gone and the remaining man, in a T-shirt and boxer briefs, stood before us.

She introduced us. "Where's Kurokawa?" she asked.

"That's the bed he was assigned," Lenox said. "I saw him last night but he didn't come to bed. He often goes out into the woods when he gets too freaked out about all the people."

"That jives with what he told us," I said. Ray and I explained about the blind he had mentioned, at the edge of the property.

"You know where that might be?" Agent Cohen asked Lenox.

"Think so. Come on over here." A large topographical map from the U.S. Geographical Survey was posted on one wall. We explained that Kurokawa had told us his blind was at the edge of the property, near a stream where white-tailed deer stopped to drink. A small stream cut across the upper left corner of the land that Duncan owned, butting up against the national forest, so that was where we decided to concentrate.

Augie Lenox said that he'd often hiked up that way, though he'd never noticed Brian's blind, and he volunteered to lead Ray and me up there to take a look. He'd been issued a rifle when he joined the compound, and he made sure it was loaded.

"Remember, he could be armed, and we want him alive," Agent Cohen said. "He'll get spooked if there are too many people out there. Your job is just reconnaissance—if you identify his location, report back here and we'll surround the area, then close in on him."

I had grown up in the woods of Waahila Ridge Park, which butted up against my parents' house in Honolulu, so I knew how to walk quietly through undergrowth. I gave Ray a quick tutorial before we started out. "Take slow, measured breaths through your nose. Pay attention to where you put your foot—look for bare dirt or live grass. Dead leaves crunch underfoot."

He nodded.

"Heel down, then roll your foot forward. Once we get close, walk on the outer edge of your foot, from heel to toe." I demonstrated, and Ray followed.

As we climbed toward the stream, the woods grew quiet and the noise from the compound faded away. A tree branch swayed as a squirrel jumped from it, and I heard the swoosh of a predatory bird in the high canopy.

We crept forward, Augie in the lead, and gradually we heard the low gurgle of a stream passing over rocks. We had deliberately approached the area from upstream, hoping that the water's noise would mask any sounds we made.

Because we were so focused on placing our feet carefully, we stopped every few feet to survey the area. We'd already descended from the peak of the hill, following the stream's trajectory, when I looked up and saw what looked like something too dark brown to be part of the leafy cover above.

I tapped Augie and Ray on the shoulder and pointed up. As we looked more closely, the outline of a wooden blind came into view. Since we were behind it, all we could see was the rear wall, but Augie had told us that most likely the blind had a low wall around the front that a hunter or birder could hide behind.

We split up then. Ray and I circled around to the right, while Augie headed to the left. We'd continue to move until we could get a look inside the blind. Then we'd turn around and meet back in this spot. If our hunch was correct and one of us spotted Kurokawa, we'd leave Ray behind as a lookout, and Augie and I would go back down to the compound and return with reinforcements.

25 – Walking Point

I led the way through the underbrush, moving slowly and trying not to startle any creatures. I felt like the Swamp Fox, using the terrain to my advantage to camouflage myself, sneaking up on our adversary. Even though we were wearing parkas and thick-soled boots, and we were a lot more heavily armed than Marion and his men had been.

We crept through the forest for about ten minutes, making a wide circle. I leaned around a tree and got a frontal view of the blind. A square wooden box, painted with a green and brown camouflage pattern, sat on a platform supported by wooden slats. The box itself was about six feet tall, with a rectangular opening under the eave. I imagined you could sit inside the box with a rifle or a camera pointed out to capture passing wildlife.

Suddenly there was a loud thump on the far side of the blind. The dead leaves rustled, and we heard grunts and punches. I gave up trying to stay quiet and rushed toward the sounds, pushing aside the underbrush. When I came around a big oak tree I saw Brian Kurokawa kneeling on the ground with his arm around Augie Lenox's neck. Augie's rifle was on the ground a few feet away.

It looked like Brian was putting pressure on Augie's carotid artery, trying to knock him out, and I charged forward, Ray right behind me.

I struggled to get a similar choke hold on Brian while Ray pried Brian's away from Augie's neck. It took us almost a minute to free Augie, and he rolled away from Brian, gasping and choking.

Ray pulled off his gloves and retrieved a pair of handcuffs from his belt. He cuffed Brian's hands behind him, then put his gloves back on.

I knelt down on the dirt and turned to Augie. "You okay?"

His face was red and he was still coughing, but he nodded. I helped him stand up, and while we were occupied Brian tried to kick back at Ray and slip away. My partner was too fast for him, and punched him in the stomach so hard Brian doubled over. "More where that came from if you keep acting up," Ray said, shaking out his hand.

We'd had our radios on silent so that we didn't accidentally alert Kurokawa, and I turned mine back on and radioed that we had Kurokawa in custody.

"There may be additional elements at loose in the woods, so travel with caution," Agent Cohen responded.

Augie led the way back down to the compound, with Ray on one side of Brian and me on the other. We made no attempt at keeping quiet, because it seemed like Brian Kurokawa was making as much noise as possible. I walked point with my Glock drawn, scanning from right to left and back again.

I was relieved when we stepped out of the woods and saw the main buildings of the compound ahead of us. A SWAT agent approached quickly, and we turned Brian over to his custody.

We found Agent Cohen in the compound's main operations room, where a map of the property hung on one wall, with a sophisticated system of cameras that monitored the front gate and the perimeter. From the scattered papers and the turned-over chair by the monitor bank, it looked like there'd been a fight to take over the room.

We briefed her on what had happened, and she arranged for Brian to be transported to Spokane along with Art Duncan and a couple of other men who Augie had indicated were part of the nuclear weapons program.

"Thanks for your help today," she said. "You guys did good work up there on the mountain."

"Our pleasure," I said. "What happened to the kids? Are they all okay?"

"A couple of the teenagers put up a bit of a fight, but they were subdued. We have social services on the way to look after the younger kids whose parents are being taken into custody."

There was nothing else for us to do, so Agent Cohen arranged for an agent to drive Ray and me back to the staging point where we'd left our rental car. While we waited for him, Ray used one of the computers to find us a flight that evening to Seattle. Then we rushed through a return to the motel, packing up and checking out, and then to the Spokane airport, where we returned the rental car and checked in for our flight.

The lack of sleep and the stress of the day caught up with me as we sat in hard plastic chairs at the gate. I couldn't stop yawning but I wanted to check in with Dom.

"We're on our way home," I said. "How's Mike doing?"

"He's doing better. He was awake yesterday afternoon for the twins, but he's still got a hell of a headache so he went back to sleep. Not sure how much of that is from the concussion and how much is a hangover, though."

"We'll be in transit for the rest of the day," I said. "I'll call if I can from the airport in Seattle."

"Don't worry, Kimo. We're taking care of him, and he should be right as rain by the time you get here."

I thanked him again, and hung up. The stress of the last couple of days hit me, and I closed my eyes for a moment. The next thing I knew Ray was elbowing me. "Time to board."

I tried to go back to sleep on the flight to Seattle but I couldn't. I kept thinking about Mike, home alone on a Friday night, drinking enough that his father would say he smelled like a brewery.

At six-four and about two hundred fifty pounds, Mike was able to have a couple of drinks without feeling adverse effects. He and I occasionally split a bottle of wine over dinner, had a couple of fruity drinks at bars, often drank a beer or two at home on a Saturday night. Sometimes we got a bit tipsy, especially if we were drinking on an empty stomach, but never incapacitated.

At least, Mike hadn't been drunk in my presence.

We had a complicated romantic history. The first time we got together, we were both pretty fresh out of the closet, and we were each other's first real boyfriend. The stress of coming out had taken its toll on us, and we'd broken up.

We'd both had a difficult time after that. I felt bad about the way things had ended, and I began a series of dangerous sexual adventures, seeking men who would punish me for my transgressions. Mike had found his refuge in alcohol, drinking to forget the love he thought he'd lost.

Several months passed, and we had to work together again, as we investigated an arson at a shopping center my father owned, where a young man was killed. We realized that we were still hung up on each other and agreed to give our relationship a second chance.

At the time, Mike attended a few meetings of Alcoholics Anonymous. He came to believe that though he'd used alcohol to soothe his aches, he wasn't an alcoholic, and had resumed drinking on a casual basis with me.

Nearly eight years had passed without a problem. Or had they? Had I ignored any warning signs? Had Mike's drinking only been kept in check because I was there with him? It was clear his judgment had been impaired—who climbs a ladder to the roof in the middle of the night?

We had to hurry through the Seattle airport to catch our flight to Honolulu and I didn't get a chance to call home again. I fell asleep almost as soon as we took off, though I squirmed restlessly, my dreams agitated. I was still exhausted and bleary when we landed, close to ten-thirty at night, and all I wanted was to go home, make sure Mike was all right, and then sleep for days.

I fidgeted as we waited for our bags. Dakota had texted me that he was outside waiting for us, and I called him. "How's Mike?" I asked.

"He looks like shit," Dakota said.

"Be more specific," I said. "What does looks like shit mean?"

Dakota groaned. "He has all these scrapes on his head, and big ugly purple bruises on his arms and legs."

"But he's okay?"

"Yes Dad," he said, drawing out the words. He only called us Dad when he was irritated with us, but I liked to hear it. If Dakota felt good enough about Mike to tease me, then things had to be all right.

The conveyor buzzed and bags began to spill out. A few minutes later we were out in the arrival terminal and I saw Dakota.

A huge lump rose in my throat. Dakota had grown up a lot since the first time I met him, as a confused teen hanging around the edges of the gay youth group I mentored at the time. Now he was almost twenty years old, a handsome kid with shoulder-length dark hair and a hipster goatee. Going to college, becoming an adult.

I hugged him hard. "Missed you," I said into his hair.

"Back at you," he said. He fist-bumped Ray. "Let's get a move on. I know you both want to get home."

He dropped Ray off first, then took me home. As he drove off, I opened the door and Roby jumped on me. "Yes, I missed you too, boy." Tears began to well in the corners of my eyes. "Where's your daddy?"

Soon-O came down the stairs. "Mike's awake," she said. "He heard the car come in and he knew it was you."

I kissed her cheek quickly, then took the stairs two at a time, eager as Roby to see the man I loved.

26 – Grown-Up Lives

Mike looked better than I expected. He was sitting up in bed with the covers pulled up, so the only damage I could see was an ugly red scrape along one side of his handsome face. I hurried over to him, leaned down, and kissed him lightly on the lips.

"I'm not broken yet," he said. "And a good kiss will do me a world of good."

I smiled, and climbed onto the bed beside him. Then I leaned in and kissed him again, this time pressing my lips against his, breathing in his scent. The faintest hint of lemon verbena soap and a light musk that was unmistakably Mike. My nose nuzzled against his and he reached up and wrapped an arm around my shoulders, pulling me even closer.

I planted one hand beside him and leaned over him, and beneath me he winced.

"What?" I pulled back immediately.

"Just a few scrapes and bruises," he said. "I'm fine. Come back."

I shook my head. "I want to see." I went over to the bedroom door, where Roby was sprawled. I gently nudged him and he scrambled up. I closed the door, leaving him out in the hallway, and turned back to Mike, who was still under the covers. "Come on. Show and tell."

"It's nothing."

I crossed my arms over my chest. "And nothing is exactly what you're going to get until I can make a full inspection."

"Playing doctor now?" he asked, with a sparkle in his eyes.

"If that's what it takes."

He pulled down the covers. As Dakota had said, there were ugly purple bruises on his arms, and another big one on his chest.

"Come on. Full Monty."

"Really?"

"Yes, really."

He got out of bed. He was wearing a pair of my boxer shorts, printed with parrots and tropical foliage, and that made my heart skip a beat. He'd missed me.

He shucked the shorts and did a couple of body-builder poses for me. The bruises on his legs were grimmer, mixed with red scrapes. "I do need to put some antibiotic ointment on these," Mike said. "Think you can give me a hand?"

"Of course." I went into the bathroom to find the ointment and when I returned, Mike was lying on top of the covers, naked and hard. He held up a tube of massage cream we kept in the bedside drawer.

"You could start with this first," he said. "And then put the ointment on when we're finished."

"Are you sure you're up for this? What about all those bruises?"

"Be gentle with me, kind sir," he said, and he smiled impishly.

While he rolled over onto his stomach, I began to shuck my clothes. When I was naked, I straddled him and began rubbing the massage cream into his shoulders. I was hard, too, and my balls rested on his back as I worked.

He moaned as I worked his stiff muscles, going lightly over the bruised spots. Then I had him roll over, and I leaned down and took his dick in my mouth. "That's the kind of Kimo-therapy I need," he said.

I had to pull off his dick for a moment to laugh, but then I went back to work.

"Turn around," he said, as I licked my way up and down his shaft. "I want to do you at the same time."

It took some contorting to find a position that worked for both of us and didn't put too much pressure on any of his bruised spots, but we were motivated enough. Slowly and carefully, we worked each other to climax. By then, Roby was whining outside the door, and I dragged my carcass up, took him downstairs and let him out in the back yard, then locked up the house and went back upstairs.

Mike was already asleep by then, and I slipped into bed beside him and went right to sleep, waking only the next morning to Roby sniffing my face.

And so it began, a slow slide back into normal routines. I took a couple of days off to rest up and look after Mike, and waited until he was feeling better to broach the subject of his drinking.

"I was lonely here, feeling sorry for myself, and I had a couple of beers. More than I should have had. Then the TV went out, and I decided to climb up on the roof to check it out."

"Ray wants to go back to Philadelphia," I blurted out. I wasn't sure why that had popped into my head, but it was all part of the discussion we had to have.

"Really? Stay with the Bureau or go back to being a detective?"

"He's still figuring it out. He and Julie want Vinnie to grow up around family."

"Family's important. We're lucky to have our ohana right here. They really kicked in when I got hurt."

"I don't want you to get hurt again," I said, leaning into him. "It scared the shit out of me when Dom called me."

"Back at you," he said. "Do you think we're both getting too old for this kind of thing?"

"You mean running into fires and chasing down bad guys?" I asked.

He nodded.

It took me a while to organize my thoughts. I'd gone to the police academy back when I was confused about my sexuality. I thought that entering a tough, macho profession would help me ignore the same-sex urges I felt.

That hadn't happened, but along the way I'd discovered a purpose for my life. To protect and serve, the HPD motto. What else could I be if I wasn't a cop?

Then I remembered how much I had enjoyed mentoring the gay teen group, back when I was single and lived in Waikiki. I had given that up when Mike and I moved in together, when I had a new relationship to nurture. Then Dakota had joined our household, and then the twins had been born.

"I might want to go back to school," I said suddenly. The idea felt like one that had been percolating in the back of my head for a long time. "To study sociology and social work. Maybe get a job with a gay organization, or a teen group."

"You'd give up being a cop?"

"I'm not sure yet. Still finding my way." I looked at him. "Any ideas about what you want to do?"

"There's an opening for an assistant chief in the operations division," Mike said. "No more running around fires. I might need to take a couple of business courses myself."

"You think we could do that?" I asked. "Sometimes I feel like we're a couple of kids, a fireman and a policeman, like those aren't really grown up jobs."

"We're both in our forties," Mike said. "Maybe this is our mid-life crisis."

"Or maybe we're both ready to grow up."

He leaned over and kissed me. "Whatever happens, as long as we're together, I know we'll be all right."

The following weekend, Sandra and Cathy brought the twins over for a small family luau in the back yard. My brothers and their families were there, and those of my nieces and nephews who were still young enough not to be away at college or pursuing their own careers. As Mike and I played with Addie and Owen, I thought about how lucky I was to have my ohana around me, and knew I'd do whatever I had to in order to protect them.

About the Author

NEIL PLAKCY is the author of the Mahu Investigation series about openly gay Honolulu homicide detective Kimo Kanapa'aka. His other books include the *Have Body, Will Guard* series, the *Golden Retriever Mysteries*, and numerous stand-alone works of romance and mystery. Sign up for Neil's newsletter at his website: www.mahubooks.com.

Reading Order for the
Mahu Investigation Series